ROSMERSHOLM
A play in four acts

by
HENRIK IBSEN

Translated by R. FARQUHARSON SHARP

DRAMATIS PERSONAE

John Rosmer, of Rosmersholm, an ex-clergyman.

Rebecca West, one of his household, originally engaged as companion to the late Mrs. Rosmer.

Kroll, headmaster of the local grammar school, Rosmer's brother-in-law.

Ulrik Brendel.

Peter Mortensgaard.

Mrs. Helseth, Rosmer's housekeeper.

(The action takes place at Rosmersholm, an old manor-house in the neighbourhood of a small town on a fjord in western Norway.)

ACT 1

(SCENE—The sitting-room at Rosmersholm; a spacious room, comfortably furnished in old-fashioned style. In the foreground, against the right-hand wall, is a stove decorated with sprigs of fresh birch and wild flowers. Farther back, a door. In the back wall folding doors leading into the entrance hall. In the left-hand wall a window, in front of which is a stand filled with flowers and plants. Near the stove stand a table, a couch and an easy-chair. The walls are hung round with portraits, dating from various periods, of clergymen, military officers and other officials in uniform. The window is open, and so are the doors into the lobby and the outer door. Through the latter is seen an avenue of old trees leading to a courtyard. It is a summer evening, after sunset. REBECCA WEST is sitting by the window crocheting a large white woollen shawl, which is nearly completed. From time to time she peeps out of window through the flowers. MRS. HELSETH comes in from the right.)

Mrs. Helseth. Hadn't I better begin and lay the table for supper, miss?

Rebecca. Yes, do. Mr. Rosmer ought to be in directly.

Mrs. Helseth. Isn't there a draught where you are sitting, miss?

Rebecca. There is a little. Will you shut up, please? (MRS. HELSETH goes to the hall door and shuts it. Then she goes to the window, to shut it, and looks out.)

Mrs. Helseth. Isn't that Mr. Rosmer coming there?

Rebecca. Where? (Gets up.) Yes, it is he. (Stands behind the window-curtain.) Stand on one side. Don't let him catch sight of us.

Mrs. Helseth (stepping back). Look, miss—he is beginning to use the mill path again.

Rebecca. He came by the mill path the day before yesterday too. (Peeps out between the curtain and the window-frame). Now we shall see whether—

Mrs. Helseth. Is he going over the wooden bridge?

Rebecca. That is just what I want to see. (After a moment.) No. He has turned aside. He is coming the other way round to-day too. (Comes away from the window.) It is a long way round.

Mrs. Helseth. Yes, of course. One can well understand his shrinking from going over that bridge. The spot where such a thing has happened is—

Rebecca (folding up her work). They cling to their dead a long time at Rosmersholm.

Mrs. Helseth. If you ask me, miss, I should say it is the dead that cling to Rosmersholm a long time.

Rebecca (looking at her). The dead?

Mrs. Helseth. Yes, one might almost say that they don't seem to be able to tear themselves away from those they have left behind.

Rebecca. What puts that idea into your head?

Mrs. Helseth. Well, otherwise I know the White Horses would not be seen here.

Rebecca. Tell me, Mrs. Helseth—what is this superstition about the White Horses?

Mrs. Helseth. Oh, it is not worth talking about. I am sure you don't believe in such things, either.

Rebecca. Do you believe in them?

Mrs. Helseth (goes to the window and shuts it). Oh, I am not going to give you a chance of laughing at me, miss. (Looks out.) See—is that not Mr. Rosmer out on the mill path again?

Rebecca (looking out). That man out there? (Goes to the window.) Why, that is Mr. Kroll, of course!

Mrs. Helseth. So it is, to be sure.

Rebecca. That is delightful, because he is certain to be coming here.

Mrs. Helseth. He actually comes straight over the wooden bridge, he does for all that she was his own sister. Well, I will go in and get the supper laid, miss. (Goes out to the right. REBECCA stands still for a moment, then waves her hand out of the window, nodding and smiling. Darkness is beginning to fall.)

Rebecca (going to the door on the right and calling through it). Mrs. Helseth, I am sure you won't mind preparing something extra nice for supper? You know what dishes Mr. Kroll is especially fond of.

Mrs. Helseth. Certainly, miss. I will.

Rebecca (opening the door into the lobby). At last, Mr. Kroll! I am so glad to see you!

Kroll (coming into the lobby and putting down his stick). Thank you. Are you sure I am not disturbing you?

Rebecca. You? How can you say such a thing?

Kroll (coming into the room). You are always so kind. (Looks round the room.) Is John up in his room?

Rebecca. No, he has gone out for a walk. He is later than usual of coming in, but he is sure to be back directly. (Points to the sofa.) Do sit down and wait for him.

Kroll (putting down his hat). Thank you. (Sits down and looks about him.) How charmingly pretty you have made the old room look! Flowers everywhere!

Rebecca. Mr. Rosmer is so fond of having fresh flowers about him.

Kroll. And so are you, I should say.

Rebecca. Yes, I am. I think their scent has such a delicious effect on one—and till lately we had to deny ourselves that pleasure, you know.

Kroll (nodding slowly). Poor Beata could not stand the scent of them.

Rebecca. Nor their colours either. They made her feel dazed.

Kroll. Yes, I remember. (Continues in a more cheerful tone of voice). Well, and how are things going here?

Rebecca. Oh, everything goes on in the same quiet, placid way. One day is exactly like another. And how are things with you? Is your wife—?

Kroll. Oh, my dear Miss West, don't let us talk about my affairs. In a family there is always something or other going awry—especially in such times as we live in now.

Rebecca (after a short pause, sitting down in an easy-chair near the sofa). Why have you never once been near us during the whole of your holidays?

Kroll. Oh, it doesn't do to be importunate, you know.

Rebecca. If you only knew how we have missed you.

Kroll. And, besides, I have been away, you know.

Rebecca. Yes, for a fortnight or so. I suppose you have been going the round of the public meetings?

Kroll (nods). Yes, what do you say to that? Would you ever have thought I would become a political agitator in my old age—eh?

Rebecca (smilingly). You have always been a little bit of an agitator, Mr. Kroll.

Kroll. Oh, yes; just for my own amusement. But for the future it is going to be in real earnest. Do you ever read the Radical newspapers?

Rebecca. Yes, I won't deny that!

Kroll. My dear Miss West, there is no objection to that—not as far as you are concerned.

Rebecca. No, that is just what I think. I must follow the course of events—keep up with what is happening.

Kroll. Well, under any circumstances, I should never expect you, as a woman, to side actively with either party in the civic dispute—indeed one might more properly call it the civil war—that is raging here. I dare say you have read, then, the abuse these "nature's gentlemen" are pleased to shower upon me, and the scandalous coarseness they consider they are entitled to make use of?

Rebecca. Yes, but I think you have held your own pretty forcibly.

Kroll. That I have—though I say it. I have tasted blood now, and I will make them realise that I am not the sort of man to take it lying down—. (Checks himself.) No, no, do not let us get upon that sad and distressing topic this evening.

Rebecca. No, my dear Mr. Kroll, certainly not.

Kroll. Tell me, instead, how you find you get on at Rosmersholm, now that you are alone here—I mean, since our poor Beata—

Rebecca. Oh, thanks—I get on very well here. Her death has made a great gap in the house in many ways, of course—and one misses her and grieves for her, naturally. But in other respects—

Kroll. Do you think you will remain here?—permanently, I mean?

Rebecca. Dear Mr. Kroll, I really never think about it at all. The fact is that I have become so thoroughly domesticated here that I almost feel as if I belonged to the place too.

Kroll. You? I should think you did!

Rebecca. And as long as Mr. Rosmer finds I can be any comfort or any use to him, I will gladly remain here, undoubtedly.

Kroll (looking at her, with some emotion). You know, there is something splendid about a woman's sacrificing the whole of her youth for others.

Rebecca. What else have I had to live for?

Kroll. At first when you came here there was your perpetual worry with that unreasonable cripple of a foster-father of yours—

Rebecca. You mustn't think that Dr. West was as unreasonable as that when we lived in Finmark. It was the trying journeys by sea that broke him up. But it is quite true that after we had moved here there were one or two hard years before his sufferings were over.

Kroll. Were not the years that followed even harder for you?

Rebecca. No; how can you say such a thing! I, who was so genuinely fond of Beata—! And she, poor soul was so sadly in need of care and sympathetic companionship.

Kroll. You deserve to be thanked and rewarded for the forbearance with which you speak of her.

Rebecca (moving a little nearer to him). Dear Mr. Kroll, you say that so kindly and so sincerely that I feel sure you really bear me no ill-will.

Kroll. Ill-will? What do you mean?

Rebecca. Well, it would not be so very surprising if it were rather painful for you to see me, a stranger, doing just as I like here at Rosmersholm.

Kroll. How in the world could you think—!

Rebecca. Then it is not so? (Holds out her hand to, him.) Thank you, Mr. Kroll; thank you for that.

Kroll. But what on earth could make you take such an idea into your head?

Rebecca. I began to be afraid it might be so, as you have so seldom been out here to see us lately.

Kroll. I can assure you, you have been on the wrong scent entirely, Miss West. And, in any case, the situation of affairs is unchanged in any essential point; because during the last sad years of poor Beata's life it was you and you alone, even then, that looked after everything here.

Rebecca. But it was more like a kind of regency in the wife's name.

Kroll. Whatever it was, I—. I will tell you what, Miss West; as far as I am concerned I should have nothing whatever to say against it if you. But it doesn't do to say such things.

Rebecca. What things?

Kroll. Well, if it so happened that you were to step into the empty place—

Rebecca. I have the place I want, already, Mr. Kroll.

Kroll. Yes, as far as material benefits go; but not—

Rebecca (interrupting him, in a serious voice). For shame, Mr. Kroll! How can you sit there and jest about such things!

Kroll. Oh, well, I dare say our good John Rosmer thinks he has had more than enough of married life. But, all the same—

Rebecca. Really, you almost make me feel inclined to laugh at you.

Kroll. All the same—Tell me, Miss West, if I may be allowed the question, how old are you?

Rebecca. I am ashamed to say I was twenty-nine on my last birthday, Mr. Kroll. I am nearly thirty.

Kroll. Quite so. And Rosmer—how old is he? Let me see. He is five years younger than me, so he must be just about forty-three. It seems to me it would be very suitable.

Rebecca. No doubt, no doubt. It would be remarkably suitable—Will you stop and have supper with us?

Kroll. Thank you. I had meant to pay you a good long visit, because there is a matter I want to talk over with our excellent friend—Well, then, Miss West, to prevent your taking foolish ideas into your head again, I will come out here again from time to time, as in the old days.

Rebecca. Yes, please do. (Holds out her hand to, him.) Thank you, thank you! You are really uncommonly good-natured.

Kroll (with a little grumble). Am I? I can tell you that is more than they say at home. (ROSMER comes in by the door on the right.)

Rebecca. Mr. Rosmer, do you see who is sitting here?

Rosmer. Mrs. Helseth told me. (KROLL gets up.) I am so glad to see you here again, my dear fellow. (Puts his hands on KROLL'S shoulders and looks him in the face.) Dear old friend! I knew that one day we should be on our old footing again.

Kroll. My dear fellow, have you that insane idea in your head too, that any thing could come between us?

Rebecca (to ROSMER). Isn't it delightful to think it was all our imagination!

Rosmer. Is that really true, Kroll? But why have you kept so obstinately away from us?

Kroll (seriously, and in, a subdued voice). Because I did not want to come here like a living reminder of the unhappy time that is past—and of her who met her death in the mill-race.

Rosmer. It was a very kind thought on your part. You are always so considerate. But it was altogether unnecessary to keep away from us on that account. Come along, let us sit down on the sofa. (They sit down.) I can assure you it is not in the least painful for me to think about Beata. We talk about her every day. She seems to us to have a part in the house still.

Kroll. Does she really?

Rebecca (lighting the lamp). Yes, it is really quite true.

Rosmer. She really does. We both think so affectionately of her. And both Rebecca—both Miss West and I know in our hearts that we did all that lay in our power for the poor afflicted creature. We have nothing to reproach ourselves with. That is why I feel there is something sweet and peaceful in the way we can think of Beata now.

Kroll. You dear good people! In future I am coming out to see you every day.

Rebecca (sitting down in an arm-chair). Yes, let us see that you keep your word.

Rosmer (with a slight hesitation). I assure you, my dear fellow, my dearest wish would be that our intimacy should never suffer in any way. You know, you have seemed to be my natural adviser as long as we have known one another, even from my student days.

Kroll. I know, and I am very proud of the privilege. Is there by any chance anything in particular just now—?

Rosmer. There are a great many things that I want very much to talk over with you frankly—things that lie very near my heart.

Rebecca. I feel that is so, too, Mr. Rosmer. It seems to me it would be such a good thing if you two old friends—

Kroll. Well, I can assure you I have even more to talk over with you—because I have become an active politician, as I dare say you know.

Rosmer. Yes, I know you have. How did that come about?

Kroll. I had to, you see, whether I liked it or not. It became impossible for me to remain an idle spectator any longer. Now that the Radicals have become so distressingly powerful, it was high time. And that is also why I have induced our little circle of friends in the town to bind themselves more definitely together. It was high time, I can tell you!

Rebecca (with a slight smile). As a matter of fact, isn't it really rather late now?

Kroll. There is no denying it would have been more fortunate if we had succeeded in checking the stream at an earlier point. But who could really foresee what was coming? I am sure I could not. (Gets up and walks up and down.) Anyway, my eyes are completely opened now; for the spirit of revolt has spread even into my school.

Rosmer. Into the school? Surely not into your school?

Kroll. Indeed it has. Into my own school. What do you think of this? I have got wind of the fact that the boys in the top class—or rather, a part of the boys in it—have formed themselves into a secret society and have been taking in Mortensgaard's paper!

Rebecca. Ah, the "Searchlight".

Kroll. Yes, don't you think that is a nice sort of intellectual pabulum for future public servants? But the saddest part of it is that it is all the most promising boys in the class that have conspired together and hatched this plot against me. It is only the duffers and dunces that have held aloof from it.

Rebecca. Do you take it so much to heart, Mr. Kroll?

Kroll. Do I take it to heart, to find myself so hampered and thwarted in my life's work? (Speaking more gently.) I might find it in my heart to say that I could even take that for what it is worth; but I have not told you the worst of it yet. (Looks round the room.) I suppose nobody is likely to be listening at the doors?

Rebecca. Oh, certainly not.

Kroll. Then let me tell you that the revolt and dissension has spread into my own home—into my own peaceful home—and has disturbed the peace of my family life.

Rosmer (getting up). Do you mean it? In your own home?

Rebecca (going up to Kroll). Dear Mr. Kroll, what has happened?

Kroll. Would you believe it that my own children—. To make a long story short, my boy Laurits is the moving spirit of the conspiracy at the school. And Hilda has embroidered a red portfolio to keep the numbers of the "Searchlight" in.

Rosmer. I should never have dreamed of such a thing; in your family—in your own house!

Kroll. No, who would ever have dreamed of such a thing? In my house, where obedience and order have always ruled—where hitherto there has never been anything but one unanimous will—

Rebecca. How does your wife take it?

Kroll. Ah, that is the most incredible part of the whole thing. She, who all her days—in great things and small—has concurred in my opinions and approved of all my views, has actually not refrained from throwing her weight on the children's side on many points. And now she considers I am to blame for what has happened. She says I try to coerce the young people too much. Just as if it were not necessary to—. Well, those are the sort of dissensions I have going on at home. But naturally I talk as little about it as possible; it is better to be silent about such things. (Walks across the floor.) Oh, yes.—Oh, yes. (Stands by the window, with his hands behind his back, and looks out.)

Rebecca (goes up to ROSMER, and speaks in low, hurried tones, unheard by KROLL). Do it!

Rosmer (in the same tone). Not to-night.

Rebecca (as before). Yes, this night of all others. (Goes away from him and adjusts the lamp.)

Kroll (coming back). Yes, my dear John, so now you know the sort of spirit of the age that has cast its shadow both over my home life and my official work. Ought I not to oppose this appalling, destructive, disorganising tendency with all the weapons I can lay my hands upon? Of course it is certainly my duty—and that both with my pen and my tongue.

Rosmer. But have you any hope that you can produce any effect in that way?

Kroll. At all events I mean to take my share in the fight as a citizen. And I consider that it is the duty of every patriotic man, every man who is concerned about what is right, to do the same. And, I may as well tell you, that is really the reason why I have come here to see you to-night.

Rosmer. My dear fellow, what do you mean? What can I—?

Kroll. You are going to help your old friends, and do as we are doing—take your share in it to the best of your ability.

Rebecca. But, Mr. Kroll, you know how little taste Mr. Rosmer has for that sort of thing.

Kroll. Then he has got to overcome that distaste now. You do not keep abreast of the times, John. You sit here and bury yourself in your historical researches. Goodness knows, I have the greatest respect for family pedigrees and all that they imply. But this is not the time for such occupations, unhappily. You have no conception of the state of affairs that is going on all over the country. Every single idea is turned upside down, or very nearly so. It will be a hard fight to get all the errors straightened out again.

Rosmer. I can quite believe it. But that sort of a fight is not in my line at all.

Rebecca. Besides, I rather fancy that Mr. Rosmer has come to look at the affairs of life with wider opened eyes than before.

Kroll (with a start). Wider opened eyes?

Rebecca. Yes, or with an opener mind—with less prejudice.

Kroll. What do you mean by that? John—surely you could never be so weak as to allow yourself to be deluded by the accidental circumstance that the demagogues have scored a temporary success!

Rosmer. My dear fellow, you know very well that I am no judge of politics; but it certainly seems to me that of late years individual thought has become somewhat more independent.

Kroll. Quite so—but do you consider that as a matter of course to be a good thing? In any case you are vastly mistaken, my friend. Just inquire a little into the opinions that are current amongst the Radicals, both out here in the country and in town. You will find them to be nothing else than the words of wisdom that appear in the "Searchlight".

Rebecca. Yes, Mortensgaard has a great deal of influence over the people about here.

Kroll. Yes, just think of it—a man with as dirty a record as his! A fellow that was turned out of his place as a schoolmaster because of his immoral conduct! This is the sort of man that poses as a leader of the people! And successfully, too!—actually successfully! I hear that he means to enlarge his paper now. I know, on reliable authority, that he is looking for a competent assistant.

Rebecca. It seems to me surprising that you and your friends do not start an opposition paper.

Kroll. That is exactly what we intend to do. This very day we have bought the "County News." There was no difficulty about the financial side of the matter; but— (Turns towards ROSMER) Now we have come to the real purport of my visit. It is the Management of it—the editorial management—that is the difficulty, you see. Look here, Rosmer—don't you feel called upon to undertake it, for the sake of the good cause?

Rosmer (in a tone of consternation). I!

Rebecca. How can you think of such a thing!

Kroll. I can quite understand your having a horror of public meetings and being unwilling to expose yourself to the mercies of the rabble that frequents them. But an editor's work, which is carried on in much greater privacy, or rather—

Rosmer. No, no, my dear fellow, you must not ask that of me.

Kroll. It would give me the greatest pleasure to have a try at work of that sort myself—only it would be quite out of the question for me; I am already saddled with such an endless number of duties. You, on the other hand, who are no longer hampered by any official duties, might—. Of course the rest of us would give you all the help in our power.

Rosmer. I cannot do it, Kroll. I am not fitted for it.

Kroll. Not fitted for it? That was just what you said when your father got you your living.

Rosmer. I was quite right; and that was why I resigned it, too.

Kroll. Well, if you only make as good an editor as you did a parson, we shall be quite satisfied.

Rosmer. My dear Kroll—once for all—I cannot do it.

Kroll. Well, then, I suppose you will give us the use of your name, at all events?

Rosmer. My name?

Kroll. Yes, the mere fact of John Rosmer's name being connected with it will be a great advantage to the paper. We others are looked upon as pronounced partisans. I myself even have the reputation of being a wicked fanatic, I am told. Therefore we cannot count upon our own names to give us any particular help in making the paper known to the misguided masses. But you, on the contrary, have always held aloof from this kind of fighting. Your gentle and upright disposition, your polished mind, your unimpeachable honour, are known to and appreciated by every one about here. And then there is the deference and respect that your former position as a clergyman ensures for you—and, besides that, there is the veneration in which your family, name is held!

Rosmer. Oh, my family name.

Kroll (pointing to the portraits). Rosmers of Rosmersholm—clergymen, soldiers, men who have filled high places in the state—men of scrupulous honour, every one of them—a family that has been rooted here, the most influential in the place, for nearly two centuries. (Lays his hand on ROSMER'S shoulder.) John, you owe it to yourself and to the traditions of your race to join us in defence of all that has hitherto been held sacred in our community. (Turning to REBECCA.) What do you say, Miss West?

Rebecca (with a quiet little laugh). my dear Mr. Kroll—it all sounds so absurdly ludicrous to me.

Kroll. What! Ludicrous?

Rebecca. Yes, because it is time you were told plainly—

Rosmer (hurriedly). No, no—don't! Not now!

Kroll (looking from one to the other). But, my dear friends, what on earth—? (Breaks off, as MRS. HELSETH comes in, by the door on the right.) Ahem!

Mrs. Helseth. There is a man at the kitchen door, sir. He says he wants to see you.

Rosmer (in a relieved voice). Is there? Well, ask him to come in.

Mrs. Helseth. Shall I show him in here, sir?

Rosmer. Certainly.

Mrs. Helseth. But he doesn't look the sort of man one ought to allow in here.

Rebecca. What does he look like, Mrs. Helseth?

Mrs. Helseth. Oh, he is not much to look at, Miss.

Rosmer. Did he not give you his name?

Mrs. Helseth. Yes, I think he said it was Hekman, or something like that.

Rosmer. I do not know any one of that name.

Mrs. Helseth. And he said his Christian name was Ulrik.

Rosmer (with a start of surprise). Ulrik Hetman! Was that it?

Mrs. Helseth. Yes, sir, it was Hetman.

Kroll. I am certain I have heard that name before.

Rebecca. Surely it was the name that strange creature used to write under—

Rosmer (to Kroll). It is Ulrik Brendel's pseudonym, you know.

Kroll. That scamp Ulrik Brendel. You are quite right.

Rebecca. So he is alive still.

Rosmer. I thought he was travelling with a theatrical company.

Kroll. The last I heard of him was that he was in the workhouse.

Rosmer. Ask him to come in, Mrs. Helseth.

Mrs. Helseth. Yes, sir. (Goes out.)

Kroll. Do you really mean to allow this fellow into your house?

Rosmer. Oh, well, you know he was my tutor once.

Kroll. I know that what he did was to stuff your head with revolutionary ideas, and that in consequence your father turned him out of the house with a horsewhip.

Rosmer (a little bitterly). Yes, my father was always the commanding officer—even at home.

Kroll. Be grateful to his memory for that, my dear John. Ah!

(MRS. HELSETH shows ULRIK BRENDEL in at the door, then goes out and shuts the door after her. BRENDEL is a good-looking man with grey hair and beard; somewhat emaciated, but active and alert; he is dressed like a common tramp, in a threadbare frock coat, shoes with holes in them, and no visible linen at his neck or wrists. He wears a pair of old black gloves, carries a dirty soft hat under his arm, and has a walking-stick in his hand. He looks puzzled at first, then goes quickly up to KROLL and holds out his hand to him.)

Brendel. Good-evening, John!

Kroll. Excuse me

Brendel. Did you ever expect to see me again? And inside these hated walls, too?

Kroll. Excuse me. (Points to ROSMER.) Over there.

Brendel (turning round). Quite right. There he is. John—my boy—my favourite pupil!

Rosmer (shaking hands with him). My old tutor!

Brendel. In spite of certain recollections, I could not pass by Rosmersholm without paying you a flying visit.

Rosmer. You are very welcome here now. Be sure of that.

Brendel. And this charming lady—? (Bows to Rebecca.) Your wife, of course.

Rosmer. Miss West.

Brendel. A near relation, I presume. And our stranger friend here? A colleague, I can see.

Rosmer. Mr. Kroll, master of the grammar school here.

Brendel. Kroll? Kroll? Wait a moment. Did you take the Philology course in your student days?

Kroll. Certainly I did.

Brendel. By Jove, I used to know you, then

Kroll. Excuse me—

Brendel. Were you not—

Kroll. Excuse me—

Brendel. —one of those champions of all the virtues that got me turned out of the Debating Society?

Kroll. Very possibly. But I disclaim any other acquaintance with you.

Brendel. All right, all right! Nach Belieben, Mr. Kroll. I dare say I shall get over it. Ulrik Brendel will still be himself in spite of it.

Rebecca. Are you on your way to the town, Mr. Brendel?

Brendel. You have hit the nail on the head, ma'am. At certain intervals I am obliged to do something for my living. I do not do it willingly—but, enfin—when needs must—

Rosmer. My dear Mr. Brendel, will you not let me be of assistance to you? In some way or another, I mean—

Brendel. Ah, what a proposal to come from you! Could you wish to soil the tie that binds us together? Never, John—never!

Rosmer. But what do you propose to do in the town, then? I assure you, you won't find it so easy—

Brendel. Leave that to me, my boy. The die is cast. The unworthy individual who stands before you is started on an extensive campaign—more extensive than all his former excursions put together. (To KROLL.) May I venture to ask you, Professor—unter uns—are there in your esteemed town any fairly decent, respectable and spacious assembly-rooms?

Kroll. The most spacious is the hall belonging to the Working Men's Association.

Brendel. May I ask, sir, if you have any special influence with that no doubt most useful Association?

Kroll. I have nothing whatever to do with it.

Rebecca (to BRENDEL). You ought to apply to Peter Mortensgaard.

Brendel. Pardon, madame—what sort of an idiot is he?

Rosmer. Why do you make up your mind he is an idiot?

Brendel. Do you suppose I can't tell, from the sound of the name, that it belongs to a plebeian?

Kroll. I did not expect that answer.

Brendel. But I will conquer my prejudices. There is nothing else for it. When a man stands at a turning-point in his life—as I do—. That is settled. I shall, put myself into communication with this person—commence direct negotiations.

Rosmer. Are you in earnest when you say you are standing at a turning-point in your life?

Brendel. Does my own boy not know that wherever Ulrik Brendel stands he is always in earnest about it? Look here, I mean to become a new man now—to emerge from the cloak of reserve in which I have hitherto shrouded myself.

Rosmer. In what way?

Brendel. I mean to take an active part in life—to step forward—to look higher. The atmosphere we breathe is heavy with storms. I want now to offer my mite upon the altar of emancipation.

Kroll. You too?

Brendel (to them all). Has your public here any intimate acquaintance with my scattered writings?

Kroll. No, I must candidly confess that—

Rebecca. I have read several of them. My foster-father had them.

Brendel. My dear lady, then you have wasted your time. They are simply trash, allow me to tell you.

Rebecca. Really?

Brendel. Those you have read, yes. My really important works no man or woman knows anything about. No one—except myself.

Rebecca. How is that?

Brendel. Because they are not yet written.

Rosmer. But, my dear Mr. Brendel—

Brendel. You know, my dear John, that I am a bit of a sybarite—a gourmet. I have always been so. I have a taste for solitary enjoyment, because in that way my enjoyment is twice—ten times—as keen. It is, like this. When I have been wrapped in a haze of golden dreams that have descended on me—when new, intoxicating, momentous thoughts have had their birth in my mind, and I have been fanned by the beat of their wings as they bore me aloft—at such moments I have transformed them into poetry, into visions, into pictures. In general outlines, that is to say.

Rosmer. Quite so.

Brendel. You cannot imagine the luxury of enjoyment I have experienced! The mysterious rapture of creation!—in, general outlines, as I said. Applause, gratitude, eulogies, crowns of laurel!—all these I have culled with full hands trembling with joy. In my secret ecstasies I have steeped myself in a happiness so, intoxicating—

Kroll. Ahem!

Rosmer. But you have never written anything of it down?

Brendel. Not a word. The thought of the dull clerk's work that it would mean has always moved me to a nauseating sense of disgust. Besides, why should I profane my own ideals when I could enjoy them, in all their purity, by myself? But now they shall be sacrificed. Honestly, I feel as a mother must do when she entrusts her young daughter to the arms of a husband. But I am going to, sacrifice them nevertheless—sacrifice them on the altar of emancipation. A series of carefully thought-out lectures, to be delivered all over the country!

Rebecca (impetuously). That is splendid of you, Mr. Brendel! You are giving up the most precious thing you possess.

Rosmer. The only thing.

Rebecca (looking meaningly at ROSMER). I wonder how many there are who would do as much—who dare do it?

Rosmer (returning her look). Who knows?

Brendel. My audience is moved. That refreshes my heart and strengthens my will—and now I shall proceed upon my task forthwith. There is one other point, though. (To KROLL.) Can you inform me, sir, whether there is an Abstainers' Society in the town? A Total Abstainers' Society? I feel sure there must be.

Kroll. There is one, at your service. I am the president.

Brendel. I could tell that as soon as I saw you! Well, it is not at all impossible that I may come to you and become a member for a week.

Kroll. Excuse me—we do not accept weekly members.

Brendel. A la bonne heure, my good sir. Ulrik Brendel has never been in the habit of forcing himself upon societies of that kind. (Turns to go) But I must not prolong my stay in this house, rich as it is in memories. I must go into the town and find some suitable lodging. I shall find a decent hotel of some kind there, I hope?

Rebecca. Will you not have something hot to drink before you go?

Brendel. Of what nature, dear lady?

Rebecca. A cup of tea, or—

Brendel. A thousand thanks to the most generous of hostesses!—but I do not like trespassing on private hospitality. (Waves his hand.) Good-bye to you all! (Goes to the door, but turns back.) Oh, by the way—John—Mr. Rosmer—will you do your former tutor a service for old friendship's sake?

Rosmer. With the greatest of pleasure.

Brendel. Good. Well, then, lend me—just for a day or two—a starched shirt.

Rosmer. Nothing more than that!

Brendel. Because, you see, I am travelling on foot—on this occasion. My trunk is being sent after me.

Rosmer. Quite so. But, in that case, isn't there anything else?

Brendel. Well, I will tell you what—perhaps you have an old, worn-out summer coat that you could spare?

Rosmer. Certainly I have.

Brendel. And if there happened to be a pair of presentable shoes that would go with the coat.

Rosmer. I am sure we can manage that, too. As soon as you let us know your address, we will send the things to you.

Brendel. Please don't think of it! No one must be put to any inconvenience on my account! I will take the trifles with me.

Rosmer. Very well. Will you come upstairs with me, then?

Rebecca. Let me go. Mrs. Helseth and I will see about it.

Brendel. I could never think of allowing this charming lady—

Rebecca. Nonsense! Come along, Mr. Brendel. (She goes out by the door on the right.)

Rosmer (holding BRENDEL back). Tell me—is there no other way I can be of service to you?

Brendel. I am sure I do not know of any. Yes, perdition seize it!—now that I come to think of it—John, do you happen to have seven or eight shillings on you?

Rosmer. I will see. (Opens his purse.) I have two half-sovereigns here.

Brendel. Oh, well, never mind. I may as well take them. I can always get change in town. Thanks, in the meantime. Remember that it was two half-sovereigns I had. Good-night, my own dear boy! Good-night to you, sir! (Goes out by the door on the right, where ROSMER takes leave of him and shuts the door after him.)

Kroll. Good heavens—and that is the Ulrik Brendel of whom people once thought that he would do great things!

Rosmer. At all events he has had the courage to live his life in his own way. I do not think that is such a small thing, after all.

Kroll. What? A life like his? I almost believe he would have the power, even now, to disturb all your ideas.

Rosmer. No, indeed. I have come to a clear understanding with myself now, upon all points.

Kroll. I wish I could believe it, my dear Rosmer. You are so dreadfully susceptible to impressions from without.

Rosmer. Let us sit down. I want to have a talk with you.

Kroll. By all means. (They sit down on the couch.)

Rosmer (after a short pause). Don't you think everything here looks very pleasant and comfortable?

Kroll. Yes, it looks very pleasant and comfortable now—and peaceful. You have made yourself a real home, Rosmer. And I have lost mine.

Rosmer. My dear fellow, do not say that. There may seem to be a rift just now, but it will heal again.

Kroll. Never, never. The sting will always remain. Things can never be as they were before.

Rosmer. I want to ask you something, Kroll. You and I have been the closest of friends now for so many years—does it seem to you conceivable that anything could destroy our friendship?

Kroll. I cannot imagine anything that could cause a breach between us. What has put that into your head?

Rosmer. Well—your attaching such tremendous importance to similarity of opinions and views.

Kroll. Certainly I do; but then we two hold pretty similar opinions at all events on the most essential points.

Rosmer (gently). No. Not any longer.

Kroll (trying to jump up from his seat). What is this?

Rosmer (restraining him). No, you must sit still. Please, Kroll.

Kroll. What does it all mean? I do not understand you. Tell me, straight out!

Rosmer. A new summer has blossomed in my heart—my eyes have regained the clearness of youth. And, accordingly, I am now standing where—

Kroll. Where? Where are you standing?

Rosmer. Where your children are standing.

Kroll. You? You! The thing is impossible! Where do you say you are standing?

Rosmer. On the same side as Laurits and Hilda.

Kroll (letting his head drop). An apostate. John Rosmer an apostate.

Rosmer. What you are calling apostasy ought to have made me feel sincerely happy and fortunate; but for all that I have suffered keenly, because I knew quite well it would cause you bitter sorrow.

Kroll. Rosmer, Rosmer, I shall never get over this. (Looks at him sadly.) To think that you, too, could bring yourself to sympathise with and join in the work of disorder and ruin that is playing havoc with our unhappy country.

Rosmer. It is the work of emancipation that I sympathise with.

Kroll. Oh yes, I know all about that. That is what it is called, by both those who are leading the people astray and by their misguided victims. But, be sure of this—you need expect no emancipation to be the result of the spirit that relies on the poisoning of the whole of our social life.

Rosmer. I do not give my allegiance to the spirit that is directing this, nor to any of those who are leading the fight. I want to try to bring men of all shades of opinion together—as many as I can reach—and bind them as closely together as I can. I want to live for and devote all the strength that is in me to one end only—to create a real public opinion in the country.

Kroll. So you do not consider that we have sufficient public opinion! I, for my part, consider that the whole lot of us are on the high road to be dragged down into the mire where otherwise only the common people would be wallowing.

Rosmer. It is just for that reason that I have made up my mind as to what should be the real task of public opinion.

Kroll. What task?

Rosmer. The task of making all our fellow-countrymen into men of nobility.

Kroll. All our fellow-countrymen—!

Rosmer. As many as possible, at all events.

Kroll. By what means?

Rosmer. By emancipating their ideas and purifying their aspirations, it seems to me.

Kroll. You are a dreamer, Rosmer. Are you going to emancipate them? Are you going to purify them?

Rosmer. No, my dear fellow—I can only try to awake the desire for it in them. The doing of it rests with themselves.

Kroll. And do you think they are capable of it?

Rosmer. Yes.

Kroll. Of their own power?

Rosmer. Yes, of their own power. There is no other that can do it.

Kroll (getting up). Is that speaking as befits a clergyman?

Rosmer. I am a clergyman no longer.

Kroll. Yes, but—what of the faith you were brought up in?

Rosmer. I have it no longer.

Kroll. You have it no longer?

Rosmer (getting up). I have given it up. I had to give it up, Kroll.

Kroll (controlling his emotion). I see. Yes, yes. The one thing implies the other. Was that the reason, then, why you left the service of the Church?

Rosmer. Yes. When my mind was clearly made up—when I felt the certainty that it Was not merely a transitory temptation, but that it was something that I would neither have the power nor the desire to dismiss from my mind—then I took that step.

Kroll. So it has been fermenting in your mind as long as that. And we—your friends—have never been allowed to know anything of it. Rosmer, Rosmer—how could you hide the sorrowful truth from us!

Rosmer. Because I considered it was a matter that only concerned myself; and therefore I did not wish to cause you and my other friends any unnecessary pain. I thought I should be able to live my life here as I have done hitherto—peacefully and happily. I wanted to read, and absorb myself in all the works that so far had been sealed books to me—to familiarise myself thoroughly with the great world of truth and freedom that has been disclosed to me now.

Kroll. An apostate. Every word you say bears witness to that. But, for all that, why have you made this confession of your secret apostasy? Or why just at the present moment?

Rosmer. You yourself have compelled me to it, Kroll.

Kroll. I? I have compelled you?

Rosmer. When I heard of your violent behaviour at public meetings—when I read the reports of all the vehement speeches you made there of all your bitter attacks upon those that were on the other side—your scornful censure of your opponents—oh, Kroll, to think that you—you—could be the man to do that!—then my eyes were opened to my imperative duty. Mankind is suffering from the strife that is going on now, and we ought to bring peace and happiness and a spirit of reconciliation into their souls. That is why I step forward now and confess myself openly for what I am—and, besides, I want to put my powers to the test, as well as others. Could not you—from your side—go with me in that, Kroll?

Kroll. Never, as long as I live, will I make any alliance with the forces of disorder in the community.

Rosmer. Well, let us at least fight with honourable weapons, since it seems we must fight.

Kroll. I can have nothing more to do with any one who does not think with me on matters of vital importance, and I owe such a man no consideration.

Rosmer. Does that apply even to me?

Kroll. You yourself have broken with me, Rosmer.

Rosmer. But does this really mean a breach between us?

Kroll. Between us! It is a breach with all those who have hitherto stood shoulder to shoulder with you. And now you must take the consequences.

(REBECCA comes in from the room on the right and opens the door wide.)

Rebecca. Well, that is done! We have started him off on the road to his great sacrifice, and now we can go in to supper. Will you come in, Mr. Kroll?

Kroll (taking his hat). Good-night, Miss West. This is no longer any place for me.

Rebecca (excitedly). What do you mean? (Shuts the door and comes nearer to the two men.) Have you told him—?

Rosmer. He knows now.

Kroll. We shall not let you slip out of our hands, Rosmer. We shall compel you to come back to us again.

Rosmer. I shall never find myself there any more.

Kroll. We shall see. You are not the man to endure standing alone.

Rosmer. I am not so entirely alone, even now. There are two of us to bear the solitude together here.

Kroll. Ah! (A suspicion appears to cross his mind.) That too! Beata's words!

Rosmer. Beata's?

Kroll (dismissing the thought from his mind). No, no—that was odious of me. Forgive me.

Rosmer. What? What do you mean?

Kroll. Think no more about it. I am ashamed of it. Forgive me—and good-bye. (Goes out by the door to the hall.)

Rosmer (following him). Kroll! We cannot end everything between us like this. I will come and see you to-morrow.

Kroll (turning round in the hall). You shall not set your foot in my house. (Takes his stick and goes.)

(ROSMER stands for a while at the open door; then shuts it and comes back into the room.)

Rosmer. That does not matter, Rebecca. We shall be able to go through with it, for all that—we two trusty friends—you and I.

Rebecca. What do you suppose he meant just now when he said he was ashamed of himself?

Rosmer. My dear girl, don't bother your head about that. He didn't even believe what he meant, himself. But I will go and see him tomorrow. Goodnight!

Rebecca. Are you going up so early to-night—after this?

Rosmer. As early to-night as I usually do. I feel such a sense of relief now that it is over. You see, my dear Rebecca, I am perfectly calm—so you take it calmly, too. Good-night.

Rebecca. Good-night, dear friend—and sleep well! (ROSMER goes out by the door to the lobby; then his footsteps are heard as he goes upstairs. REBECCA goes to the wall and rings a bell, which is answered by MRS. HELSETH.) You can clear the table again, Mrs. Helseth. Mr. Rosmer does not want anything, and Mr. Kroll has gone home.

Mrs. Helseth. Gone home? What was wrong with him, miss?

Rebecca (taking up her crochet-work). He prophesied that there was a heavy storm brewing—

Mrs. Helseth. That is very strange, miss, because there isn't a scrap of cloud in the sky.

Rebecca. Let us hope he doesn't meet the White Horse. Because I am afraid it will not be long before we hear something of the family ghost.

Mrs. Helseth. God forgive you, miss—don't talk of such a dreadful thing!

Rebecca. Oh, come, come!

Mrs. Helseth (lowering her voice). Do you really think, miss, that some one here is to go soon?

Rebecca. Not a bit of it. But there are so many sorts of white horses in this world, Mrs. Helseth—Well, good-night. I shall go to my room now.

Mrs. Helseth. Good-night, miss. (Rebecca takes her work and goes out to the right. MRS. HELSETH shakes her head, as she turns down the lamp, and mutters to herself): Lord—Lord!—how queer Miss West does talk sometimes!

ACT II

(SCENE. ROSMER'S study. The door into it is in the left-hand wall. At the back of the room is a doorway with a curtain drawn back from it, leading to his bedroom. On the right, a window, in front of which is a writing-table strewn with books and papers. Bookshelves and cupboards on the walls. Homely furniture. On the left, an old-fashioned sofa with a table in front of it. ROSMER, wearing a smoking-jacket, is sitting at the writing-table on a high-backed chair. He is cutting and turning over the leaves of a magazine, and dipping into it here and there. A knock is heard at the door on the left.)

Rosmer (without turning round). Come in.

(REBECCA comes in, wearing a morning wrapper.)

Rebecca. Good morning.

Rosmer (still turning over the leaves of his book). Good morning, dear. Do you want anything?

Rebecca. Only to ask if you have slept well?

Rosmer. I went to sleep feeling so secure and happy. I did not even dream. (Turns round.) And you?

Rebecca. Thanks, I got to sleep in the early morning.

Rosmer. I do not think I have felt so light-hearted for a long time as I do to-day. I am so glad that I had the opportunity to say what I did.

Rebecca. Yes, you should not have been silent so long, John.

Rosmer. I cannot understand how I came to be such a coward.

Rebecca. I am sure it was not really from cowardice.

Rosmer. Yes, indeed. I can see that at bottom there was some cowardice about it.

Rebecca. So much the braver of you to face it as you did. (Sits down beside him on a chair by the writing-table.) But now I want to confess something that I have done—something that you must not be vexed with me about.

Rosmer. Vexed? My dear girl, how can you think—?

Rebecca. Yes, because I dare say it was a little presumptuous of me, but—

Rosmer. Well, let me hear what it was.

Rebecca. Last night, when that Ulrick Brendel was going, I wrote him a line or two to take to Mortensgaard.

Rosmer (a little doubtfully). But, my dear Rebecca—What did you write, then?

Rebecca. I wrote that he would be doing you a service if he would interest himself a little in that unfortunate man, and help him in any way he could.

Rosmer. My dear, you should not have done that. You have only done Brendel harm by doing so. And besides, Mortensgaard is a man I particularly wish to have nothing to do with. You know I have been at loggerheads once with him already.

Rebecca. But do you not think that now it might be a very good thing if you got on to good terms with him again?

Rosmer. I? With Mortensgaard? For what reason, do you mean?

Rebecca. Well, because you cannot feel altogether secure now—since this has come between you and your friends.

Rosmer (looking at her and shaking his head). Is it possible that you think either Kroll or any of the others would take a revenge on me—that they could be capable of—

Rebecca. In their first heat of indignation dear. No one can be certain of that. I think, after the way Mr. Kroll took it—

Rosmer. Oh, you ought to know him better than that. Kroll is an honourable man, through and through. I will go into town this afternoon, and have a talk with him. I will have a talk with them all. Oh, you will see how smoothly everything will go. (MRS. HELSETH comes in by the door on the left.)

Rebecca (getting up). What is it, Mrs. Helseth?

Mrs. Helseth. Mr. Kroll is downstairs in the hall, miss.

Rosmer (getting up quickly). Kroll!

Rebecca. Mr. Kroll! What a surprise!

Mrs. Helseth. He asks if he may come up and speak to Mr. Rosmer.

Rosmer (to REBECCA). What did I say! (To MRS. HELSETH). Of course he may. (Goes to the door and calls down the stairs.) Come up, my dear fellow! I am delighted to see you! (He stands holding the door open. MRS. HELSETH goes out. REBECCA draws the curtain over the doorway at the back, and then begins to tidy the room. KROLL comes in with his hat in his hand.)

Rosmer (quietly, and with some emotion). I knew quite well it would not be the last time—

Kroll. To-day I see the matter in quite a different light from yesterday.

Rosmer. Of course you do, Kroll! Of course you do! You have been thinking things over—

Kroll. You misunderstand me altogether. (Puts his hat down on the table.) It is important that I should speak to you alone.

Rosmer. Why may not Miss West—?

Rebecca. No, no, Mr. Rosmer. I will go.

Kroll (looking meaningly at her). And I see I ought to apologise to you, Miss West, for coming here so early in the morning. I see I have taken you by surprise, before you have had time to—

Rebecca (with a start). Why so? Do you find anything out of place in the fact of my wearing a morning wrapper at home here?

Kroll. By no means! Besides, I have no knowledge of what customs may have grown up at Rosmersholm.

Rosmer. Kroll, you are not the least like yourself to-day.

Rebecca. I will wish you good morning, Mr. Kroll. (Goes out to the left.)

Kroll. If. you will allow me— (Sits down on the couch.)

Rosmer. Yes, my dear fellow, let us make ourselves comfortable and have a confidential talk. (Sits down on a chair facing KROLL.)

Kroll. I have not been able to close an eye since yesterday. I lay all night, thinking and thinking.

Rosmer. And what have you got to say to day?

Kroll. It will take me some time, Rosmer. Let me begin with a sort of introduction. I can give you some news of Ulrick Brendel.

Rosmer. Has he been to see you?

Kroll. No. He took up his quarters in a low-class tavern—in the lowest kind of company, of course; drank, and stood drinks to others, as long as he had any money left; and then began to abuse the whole lot of them as a contemptible rabble—and, indeed, as far as that goes he was quite right. But the result was, that he got a thrashing and was thrown out into the gutter.

Rosmer. I see he is altogether incorrigible.

Kroll. He had pawned the coat you gave him, too, but that is going to be redeemed for him. Can you guess by whom?

Rosmer. By yourself, perhaps?

Kroll. No. By our noble friend Mr. Mortensgaard.

Rosmer. Is that so?

Kroll. I am informed that Mr. Brendel's first visit was paid to the "idiot" and "plebeian".

Rosmer. Well, it was very lucky for him—

Kroll. Indeed it was. (Leans over the table, towards ROSMER.) Now I am coming to a matter of which, for the sake of our old—our former—friendship, it is my duty to warn you.

Rosmer. My dear fellow, what is that?

Kroll. It is this; that certain games are going on behind your back in this house.

Rosmer. How can you think that? Is it Rebec—is it Miss West you are alluding to?

Kroll. Precisely. And I can quite understand it on her part; she has been accustomed, for such a long time now, to do as she likes here. But nevertheless—

Rosmer. My dear Kroll, you are absolutely mistaken. She and I have no secrets from one another about anything whatever.

Kroll. Then has she confessed to you that she has been corresponding with the editor of the "Searchlight"?

Rosmer. Oh, you mean the couple of lines she wrote to him on Ulrik Brendel's behalf?

Kroll. You have found that out, then? And do you approve of her being on terms of this sort with that scurrilous hack, who almost every week tries to pillory me for my attitude in my school and out of it?

Rosmer. My dear fellow, I don't suppose that side of the question has ever occurred to her. And in any case, of course she has entire freedom of action, just as I have myself.

Kroll. Indeed? Well, I suppose that is quite in accordance with the new turn your views have taken—because I suppose Miss West looks at things from the same standpoint as you?

Rosmer. She does. We two have worked our way forward in complete companionship.

Kroll (looking at him and shaking his head slowly). Oh, you blind, deluded man!

Rosmer. I? What makes you say that?

Kroll. Because I dare not—I WILL not—think the worst. No, no, let me finish what I want to say. Am I to believe that you really prize my friendship, Rosmer? And my respect, too? Do you?

Rosmer. Surely I need not answer that question.

Kroll. Well, but there are other things that require answering—that require full explanation on your part. Will you submit to it if I hold a sort of inquiry—?

Rosmer. An inquiry?

Kroll. Yes, if I ask you questions about one or two things that it may be painful for you to recall to mind. For instance, the matter of your apostasy—well, your emancipation, if you choose to call it so—is bound up with so much else for which, for your own sake, you ought to account to me.

Rosmer. My dear fellow, ask me about anything you please. I have nothing to conceal.

Kroll. Well, then, tell me this—what do you yourself believe was the real reason of Beata's making away with herself?

Rosmer. Can you have any doubt? Or perhaps I should rather say, need one look for reasons for what an unhappy sick woman, who is unaccountable for her actions, may do?

Kroll. Are you certain that Beata was so entirely unaccountable for her actions? The doctors, at all events, did not consider that so absolutely certain.

Rosmer. If the doctors had ever seen her in the state in which I have so often seen her, both night and day, they would have had no doubt about it.

Kroll. I did not doubt it either, at the time.

Rosmer. Of course not. It was impossible to doubt it, unfortunately. You remember what I told you of her ungovernable, wild fits of passion—which she expected me to reciprocate. She terrified me! And think how she tortured herself with baseless self-reproaches in the last years of her life!

Kroll. Yes, when she knew that she would always be childless.

Rosmer. Well, think what it meant—to be perpetually in the clutches of such— agony of mind over a thing that she was not in the slightest degree responsible for—! Are you going to suggest that she was accountable for her actions?

Kroll. Hm!—Do you remember whether at that time you had, in the house any books dealing with the purport of marriage—according to the advanced views of to-day?

Rosmer. I remember Miss West's lending me a work of the kind. She inherited Dr. West's library, you know. But, my dear Kroll, you surely do not suppose that we were so imprudent as to let the poor sick creature get wind of any such ideas? I can solemnly swear that we were in no way to blame. It was the overwrought nerves of her own brain that were responsible for these frantic aberrations.

Kroll. There is one thing, at any rate, that I can tell you now, and that is that your poor tortured and overwrought Beata put an end to her own life in order that yours might be happy—and that you might be free to live as you pleased.

Rosmer (starting half up from his chair). What do you mean by that?

Kroll. You must listen to me quietly, Rosmer—because now I can speak of it. During the last year of her life she came twice to see me, to tell me what she suffered from her fears and her despair.

Rosmer. On that point?

Kroll. No. The first time she came she declared that you were on the high road to apostasy—that you were going to desert the faith that your father had taught you.

Rosmer (eagerly). What you say is impossible, Kroll!—absolutely impossible! You must be wrong about that.

Kroll. Why?

Rosmer. Because as long as Beata lived I was still doubting and fighting with myself. And I fought out that fight alone and in the completest secrecy. I do not imagine that even Rebecca—

Kroll. Rebecca?

Rosmer. Oh, well—Miss West. I call her Rebecca for the sake of convenience.

Kroll. So I have observed.

Rosmer. That is why it is so incomprehensible to me that Beata should have had any suspicion of it. Why did she never speak to me about it?—for she never did, by a single word.

Kroll. Poor soul—she begged and implored me to speak to you.

Rosmer. Then why did you never do so?

Kroll. Do you think I had a moment's doubt, at that time, that her mind was unhinged? Such an accusation as that, against a man like you! Well, she came to see me again, about a month later. She seemed calmer then; but, as she was going away, she said: "They may expect to see the White Horse soon at Rosmersholm."

Rosmer. Yes, I know—the White Horse. She often used to talk about that.

Kroll. And then, when I tried to distract her from such unhappy thoughts, she only answered: "I have not much time left; for John must marry Rebecca immediately now."

Rosmer (almost speechless). What are you saying! I marry—!

Kroll. That was on a Thursday afternoon. On the Saturday evening she threw herself from the footbridge into the millrace.

Rosmer. And you never warned us!

Kroll. Well, you know yourself how constantly she used to say that she was sure she would die before long.

Rosmer. Yes, I know. But, all the same, you ought to have warned us!

Kroll. I did think of doing so. But then it was too late.

Rosmer. But since then, why have you not—? Why have you kept all this to yourself?

Kroll. What good would it have done for me to come here and add to your pain and distress? Of course I thought the whole thing was merely wild, empty fancy—until yesterday evening.

Rosmer. Then you do not think so any longer?

Kroll. Did not Beata see clearly enough, when she saw that you were going to fall away from your childhood's faith?

Rosmer (staring in front of him). Yes, I cannot understand that. It is the most incomprehensible thing in the world to me.

Kroll. Incomprehensible or not, the thing is true. And now I ask you, Rosmer, how much truth is there in her other accusation?—the last one, I mean.

Rosmer. Accusation? Was that an accusation, then?

Kroll. Perhaps you did not notice how it was worded. She said she meant to stand out of the way. Why? Well?

Rosmer. In order that I might marry Rebecca, apparently.

Kroll. That was not quite how it was worded. Beata expressed herself differently. She said "I have not much time left; for John must marry Rebecca IMMEDIATELY now."

Rosmer (looks at him for a moment; then gets up). Now I understand you, Kroll.

Kroll. And if you do? What answer have you to make?

Rosmer (in an even voice, controlling himself). To such an unheard-of—? The only fitting answer would be to point to the door.

Kroll (getting up). Very good.

Rosmer (standing face to face with him). Listen to me. For considerably more than a year to be precise, since Beata's death—Rebecca West and I have lived here alone at Rosmersholm. All that time you have known of the charge Beata made against us; but I have never for one moment seen you appear the least scandalised at our living together here.

Kroll. I never knew, till yesterday evening, that it was a case of an apostate man and an "emancipated" woman living together.

Rosmer. Ah! So then you do not believe in any purity of life among apostates or emancipated folk? You do not believe that they may have the instinct of morality ingrained in their natures?

Kroll. I have no particular confidence in the kind of morality that is not rooted in the Church's faith.

Rosmer. And you mean that to apply to Rebecca and myself?—to my relations with Rebecca?

Kroll. I cannot make any departure, in favour of you two, from my opinion that there is certainly no very wide gulf between free thinking and—ahem!

Rosmer. And what?

Kroll. And free love, since you force me to say it.

Rosmer (gently). And you are not ashamed to say that to me!—you, who have known me ever since I was a boy.

Kroll. It is just for that reason. I know how easily you allow yourself to be influenced by those you associate with. And as for your Rebecca—well, your Miss West, then—to tell the truth, we know very little about her. To cut the matter short, Rosmer—I am not going to give you up. And you, on your part, ought to try and save yourself in time.

Rosmer. Save myself? How—? (MRS. HELSETH looks in through the door on the left.) What do you want?

Mrs. Helseth. I wanted to ask Miss West to come down, sir.

Rosmer. Miss West is not up here.

Mrs. Helseth. Indeed, sir? (Looks round the room.) That is very strange. (Goes out.)

Rosmer. You were saying—?

Kroll. Listen to me. As to what may have gone on here in secret while Beata was alive, and as to what may be still going on here, I have no wish to inquire more closely. You were, of course, extremely unhappy in your marriage—and to some extent that may be urged in your excuse—

Rosmer. Oh, how little you really know me!

Kroll. Do not interrupt me. What I want to say is this. If you definitely must continue living with Miss West, it is absolutely necessary that you should conceal the revolution of opinion—I mean the distressing apostasy—that she has beguiled you into. Let me speak! Let me speak! I say that, if you are determined to go on with this folly, for heaven's sake hold any variety of ideas or opinions or beliefs you like—but keep your opinions to yourself. It is a purely personal matter, and there is not the slightest necessity to go proclaiming it all over the countryside.

Rosmer. It is a necessity for me to abandon a false and equivocal position.

Kroll. But you have a duty towards the traditions of your family, Rosmer! Remember that! From time immemorial Rosmersholm has been a stronghold of discipline and order, of respect and esteem for all that the best people in our community have upheld and sanctioned. The whole neighbourhood has taken its tone from Rosmersholm. If the report gets about that you yourself have broken with what I may call the Rosmer family tradition, it will evoke an irreparable state of unrest.

Rosmer. My dear Kroll, I cannot see the matter in that light. It seems to me that it is my imperative duty to bring a little light and happiness into the place where the race of Rosmers has spread darkness and oppression for all these long years.

Kroll (looking severely at him). Yes, that would be a worthy action for the man with whom the race will disappear. Let such things alone, my friend. It is no suitable task for you. You were meant to lead the peaceful life of a student.

Rosmer. Yes, that may be so. But nevertheless I want to try and play my humble part in the struggles of life.

Kroll. The struggles of life! Do you know what that will mean for you? It will mean war to the death with all your friends.

Rosmer (quietly). I do not imagine they are all such fanatics as you.

Kroll. You are a simple-minded creature, Rosmer—an inexperienced creature. You have no suspicion of the violence of the storm that will burst upon you. (MRS. HELSETH slightly opens the door on the left.)

Mrs. Helseth. Miss West wishes me to ask you, sir

Rosmer. What is it?

Mrs. Helseth. There is some one downstairs that wishes to speak to you for a minute, sir.

Rosmer. Is it the gentleman that was here yesterday afternoon, by any chance?

Mrs. Helseth. No, it is that Mr. Mortensgaard.

Rosmer. Mortensgaard?

Kroll. Aha! So matters have got as far as that already, have they!

Rosmer. What does he want with me? Why did you not send him away?

Mrs. Helseth. Miss West told me to ask you if he might come up.

Rosmer. Tell him I am engaged, and—

Kroll (to MRS. HELSETH). No; show him up, please. (MRS. HELSETH goes out. KROLL takes up his hat.) I quit the field—temporarily. But we have not fought the decisive action yet.

Rosmer. As truly as I stand here, Kroll, I have absolutely nothing to do with Mortensgaard.

Kroll. I do not believe you any longer on any point. Under no circumstances shall I have any faith in you after this. It is war to the knife now. We shall try if we cannot make you powerless to do any harm.

Rosmer. Oh, Kroll—how you have sunk! How low you have sunk!

Kroll. I? And a man like you has the face to say so? Remember Beata!

Rosmer. Are you harking back to that again!

Kroll. No. You must solve the riddle of the millrace as your conscience will allow you—if you have any conscience still left. (PETER MORTENSGAARD comes in softly and quietly, by the door on the left. He is a short, slightly built man with sparse reddish hair and beard. KROLL gives him a look of hatred.) The "Searchlight" too, I see. Lighted at Rosmersholm! (Buttons up his coat.) That leaves me no doubt as to the course I should steer.

Mortensgaard (quietly). The "Searchlight" will always be ready burning to light Mr. Kroll home.

Kroll. Yes, you have shown me your goodwill for a long time. To be sure there is a Commandment that forbids us to bear false witness against our neighbour—

Mortensgaard. Mr. Kroll has no need to instruct me in the Commandments.

Kroll. Not even in the sixth?

Rosmer. Kroll—!

Mortensgaard. If I needed such instruction, Mr. Rosmer is the most suitable person to give it me.

Kroll (with scarcely concealed scorn). Mr. Rosmer? Oh yes, the Reverend Mr. Rosmer is undoubtedly the most suitable man for that! I hope you will enjoy yourselves, gentlemen. (Goes out and slams the door after him.)

Rosmer (stands looking at the door, and says to himself). Yes, yes—it had to be so. (Turns round.) Will you tell me, Mr. Mortensgaard, what has brought you out here to see me?

Mortensgaard. It was really Miss West I wanted to see. I thought I ought to thank her for the kind letter I received from her yesterday.

Rosmer. I know she has written to you. Have you had a talk with her?

Mortensgaard. Yes, a little. (Smiles slightly.) I hear that there has been a change of views in certain respects at Rosmersholm.

Rosmer. My views have changed to a very considerable extent; I might almost say entirely.

Mortensgaard. That is what Miss West said. And that was why she thought I ought to come up and have a little chat with you about this.

Rosmer. About what, Mr. Mortensgaard?

Mortensgaard. May I have your permission to announce in the "Searchlight" that you have altered your opinions, and are going to devote yourself to the cause of free thought and progress?

Rosmer. By all means. I will go so far as to ask you to make the announcement.

Mortensgaard. Then it shall appear to-morrow. It will be a great and weighty piece of news that the Reverend Mr. Rosmer of Rosmersholm has made up his mind to join the forces of light in that direction too.

Rosmer. I do not quite understand you.

Mortensgaard. What I mean is that it implies the gain of strong moral support for our party every time we win over an earnest, Christian-minded adherent.

Rosmer (with some astonishment). Then you don't know—? Did Miss West not tell you that as well?

Mortensgaard. What, Mr. Rosmer? Miss West was in a considerable hurry. She told me to come up, and that I would hear the rest of it from yourself.

Rosmer. Very well, then; let me tell you that I have cut myself free entirely—on every side. I have now, no connection of any kind with the tenets of the Church. For the future such matters have not the smallest signification for me.

Mortensgaard (looking at him in perplexity). Well, if the moon had fallen down from the sky, I could not be more—! To think that I should ever hear you yourself renounce—!

Rosmer. Yes, I stand now where you have stood for a long time. You can announce that in the "Searchlight" to-morrow too.

Mortensgaard. That, too? No, my dear Mr. Rosmer—you must excuse me—but it is not worth touching on that side of the matter.

Rosmer. Not touch on it?

Mortensgaard. Not at first, I think.

Rosmer. But I do not understand—

Mortensgaard. Well, it is like this, Mr. Rosmer. You are not as familiar with all the circumstances of the case as I am, I expect. But if you, too, have joined the forces of freedom—and if you, as Miss West says you do, mean to take part in the movement—I conclude you do so with the desire to be as useful to the movement as you possibly can, in practice as well as, in theory.

Rosmer. Yes, that is my most sincere wish.

Mortensgaard. Very well. But I must impress on you, Mr. Rosmer, that if you come forward openly with this news about your defection from the Church, you will tie your own hands immediately.

Rosmer. Do you think so?

Mortensgaard. Yes, you may be certain that there is not much that you would be able to do hereabouts. And besides, Mr. Rosmer, we have quite enough freethinkers already—indeed, I was going to say we have too many of those gentry. What the party needs is a Christian element—something that every one must respect. That is what we want badly. And for that reason it is most advisable that you should hold your tongue about any matters that do not concern the public. That is my opinion.

Rosmer. I see. Then you would not risk having anything to do with me if I were to confess my apostasy openly?

Mortensgaard (shaking his head). I should not like to, Mr. Rosmer. Lately I have made it a rule never to support anybody or anything that is opposed to the interests of the Church.

Rosmer. Have you, then, entered the fold of the Church again lately?

Mortensgaard. That is another matter altogether.

Rosmer. Oh, that is how it is. Yes, I understand you now.

Mortensgaard. Mr. Rosmer—you ought to remember that I, of all people, have not absolute freedom of action.

Rosmer. What hampers you?

Mortensgaard. What hampers me is that I am a marked man.

Rosmer. Ah—of course.

Mortensgaard. A marked man, Mr. Rosmer. And you, of all people, ought to remember that—because you were responsible, more than any one else, for my being branded.

Rosmer. If I had stood then where I stand now, I should have handled the affair more judiciously.

Mortensgaard. I think so too. But it is too late now; you have branded me, once for all—branded me for life. I do not suppose you can fully realise what such a thing means. But it is possible that you may soon feel the smart of it yourself now, Mr. Rosmer.

Rosmer. I?

Mortensgaard. Yes. You surely do not suppose that Mr. Kroll and his gang will be inclined to forgive a rupture such as yours? And the "County News" is going to be pretty bloodthirsty, I hear. It may very well come to pass that you will be a marked man, too.

Rosmer. On personal grounds, Mr. Mortensgaard, I feel myself to be invulnerable. My conduct does not offer any point of attack.

Mortensgaard (with a quiet smile). That is saying a good deal, Mr. Rosmer.

Rosmer. Perhaps it is. But I have the right to say as much.

Mortensgaard. Even if you were inclined to overhaul your conduct as thoroughly as you once overhauled mine?

Rosmer. You say that very strangely. What are you driving at?—is it anything definite?

Mortensgaard. Yes, there is one definite thing—no more than a single one. But it might be quite awkward enough if malicious opponents got a hint of it.

Rosmer. Will you have the kindness to tell me what on earth it is?

Mortensgaard. Can you not guess, Mr. Rosmer?

Rosmer. No, not for a moment.

Mortensgaard. All right. I must come out with it, then. I have in my possession a remarkable letter, that was written here at Rosmersholm.

Rosmer. Miss West's letter, you mean? Is it so remarkable?

Mortensgaard. No, that letter is not remarkable. But I received a letter from this house on another occasion.

Rosmer. From Miss West?

Mortensgaard. No, Mr. Rosmer.

Rosmer. Well, from whom, then? From whom?

Mortensgaard. From your late wife.

Rosmer. From my wife? You had a letter from my wife?

Mortensgaard. Yes, I did.

Rosmer. When?

Mortensgaard. It was during the poor lady's last days. It must be about a year and a half ago now. And that is the letter that is so remarkable.

Rosmer. Surely you know that my wife's mind was affected at that time?

Mortensgaard. I know there were a great many people who thought so. But, in my opinion, no one would have imagined anything of the kind from the letter. When I say the letter is a remarkable one, I mean remarkable in quite another way.

Rosmer. And what in the world did my poor wife find to write to you about?

Mortensgaard. I have the letter at home. It begins more or less to the effect that she is living in perpetual terror and dread, because of the fact that there are so many evilly disposed people about her whose only desire is to do you harm and mischief.

Rosmer. Me?

Mortensgaard. Yes, so she says. And then follows the most remarkable part of it all. Shall I tell you, Mr. Rosmer?

Rosmer. Of course! Tell me everything, without any reserve.

Mortensgaard. The poor lady begs and entreats me to be magnanimous. She says that she knows it was you, who got me dismissed from my post as schoolmaster, and implores me most earnestly not to revenge myself upon you.

Rosmer. What way did she think you could revenge yourself, then?

Mortensgaard. The letter goes on to say that if I should hear that anything sinful was going on at Rosmersholm, I was not to believe a word of it; that it would be only the work of wicked folk who were spreading the rumours on purpose to do you harm.

Rosmer. Does the letter say that?

Mortensgaard. You may read it at your convenience, Mr. Rosmer.

Rosmer. But I cannot understand—? What did she imagine there could be any wicked rumours about?

Mortensgaard. In the first place, that you had broken away from the faith of your childhood. Mrs. Rosmer denied that absolutely—at that time. And, in the next place—ahem!

Rosmer. In the next place?

Mortensgaard. Well, in the next place she writes—though rather confusedly—that she has no knowledge of any sinful relations existing at Rosmersholm; that she has never been wronged in any way; and that if any rumours of that sort should get about, she entreats me not to allude to them in the "Searchlight".

Rosmer. Does she mention any names?

Mortensgaard. No.

Rosmer. Who brought you the letter?

Mortensgaard. I promised not to tell that. It was brought to me one evening after dark.

Rosmer. If you had made inquiries at the time, you would have learnt that my poor unhappy wife was not fully accountable for her actions.

Mortensgaard. I did make inquiries, Mr. Rosmer; but I must say I did not get exactly that impression.

Rosmer. Not?—But why have you chosen this moment to enlighten me as to the existence of this old crazy letter?

Mortensgaard. With the object of advising you to be extremely cautious, Mr. Rosmer.

Rosmer. As to my way of life, do you mean?

Mortensgaard. Yes. You must remember that for the future you will not be unassailable.

Rosmer. So you persist in thinking that I have something to conceal here?

Mortensgaard. I do not see any reason why a man of emancipated ideas should refrain from living his life as fully as possible. Only, as I have already said, you should be cautious in future. If rumours should get about of anything that offends people's prejudices, you may be quite certain that the whole cause of freedom of thought will suffer for it. Good-bye, Mr. Rosmer.

Rosmer. Good-bye.

Mortensgaard. I shall go straight to the printing-office now and have the great piece of news inserted in the "Searchlight".

Rosmer. Put it all in.

Mortensgaard. I will put in as much as there is any need for the public to know. (Bows, and goes out. ROSMER stands at the door, while MORTENSGAARD goes downstairs. The front door is heard shutting.)

Rosmer (still standing in the doorway, calls softly). Rebecca! Reb—ahem! (Calls loudly.) Mrs. Helseth—is Miss West downstairs?

Mrs. Helseth (from below). No, sir, she is not here.

(The curtain at the end of the room is drawn back, disclosing REBECCA standing in the doorway.)

Rebecca. John!

Rosmer (turning round). What! Were you in there, in my bedroom! My dear, what were you doing there?

Rebecca (going up to him). I have been listening.

Rosmer. Rebecca! Could you do a thing like that?

Rebecca. Indeed I could. It was so horrid the way he said that—about my morning wrapper.

Rosmer. Ah, so you were in there too when Kroll—?

Rebecca. Yes. I wanted to know what was at the bottom of his mind.

Rosmer. You know I would have told you.

Rebecca. I scarcely think you would have told me everything—certainly not in his own words.

Rosmer. Did you hear everything, then?

Rebecca. Most of it, I think. I had to go down for a moment when Mortensgaard came.

Rosmer. And then came up again?

Rebecca. Do not take it ill of me, dear friend.

Rosmer. Do anything that you think right and proper. You have full freedom of action.—But what do you say to it all, Rebecca? Ah, I do not think I have ever stood so much in need of you as I do to-day.

Rebecca. Surely both you and I have been prepared for what would happen some day.

Rosmer. No, no—not for this.

Rebecca. Not for this?

Rosmer. It is true that I used to think that sooner or later our beautiful pure friendship would come to be attacked by calumny and suspicion—not on Kroll's part, for I never would have believed such a thing of him—but on the part of the coarse-minded and ignoble-eyed crowd. Yes, indeed; I had good reason enough for so jealously drawing a veil of concealment over our compact. It was a dangerous secret.

Rebecca. Why should we pay any heed to what all these other people think? You and I know that we have nothing to reproach ourselves with.

Rosmer. I? Nothing to reproach myself with? It is true enough that I thought so until to-day. But now, now, Rebecca—

Rebecca. Yes? Now?

Rosmer. How am I to account to myself for Beata's horrible accusation?

Rebecca (impetuously). Oh, don't talk about Beata! Don't think about Beata any more! She is dead, and you seemed at last to have been able to get away from the thought of her.

Rosmer. Since I have learnt of this, it seems just as if she had come to life again in some uncanny fashion.

Rebecca. Oh no—you must not say that, John! You must not!

Rosmer. I tell you it is so. We must try and get to the bottom of it. How can she have strayed into such a woeful misunderstanding of me?

Rebecca. Surely you too are not beginning to doubt that she was very nearly insane?

Rosmer. Well, I cannot deny it is just of that fact that I feel I cannot be so altogether certain any longer. And besides if it were so—

Rebecca. If it were so? What then?

Rosmer. What I mean is—where are we to look for the actual cause of her sick woman's fancies turning into insanity?

Rebecca. What good can it possibly do for you to indulge in such speculations!

Rosmer. I cannot do otherwise, Rebecca. I cannot let this doubt go on gnawing at my heart, however unwilling I may be to face it.

Rebecca. But it may become a real danger to you to be perpetually dwelling on this one lugubrious topic.

Rosmer (walking about restlessly and absorbed in the idea). I must have betrayed myself in some way or other. She must have noticed how happy I began to feel from the day you came to us.

Rebecca. Yes; but dear, even if that were so—

Rosmer. You may be sure she did not fail to notice that we read the same books; that we sought one another's company, and discussed every new topic together. But I cannot understand it—because I was always so careful to spare her. When I look back, it seems to me that I did everything I could to keep her apart from our lives. Or did I not, Rebecca?

Rebecca. Yes, yes—undoubtedly you did.

Rosmer. And so did you, too. And notwithstanding that—! Oh, it is horrible to think of! To think that here she was—with her affection all distorted by illness—never saying a word—watching us—noticing everything and—and—misconstruing everything.

Rebecca (wringing her hands). Oh, I never ought to have come to Rosmersholm.

Rosmer. Just think what she must have suffered in silence! Think of all the horrible things her poor diseased brain must have led her to believe about us and store up in her mind about us! Did she never speak to you of anything that could give you any kind of clue?

Rebecca (as if startled). To me! Do you suppose I should have remained here a day longer, if she had?

Rosmer. No, no—that is obvious. What a fight she must have fought—and fought alone, Rebecca! In despair, and all alone. And then, in the end, the poignant misery of her victory—which was also her accusation of us—in the mill-race! (Throws himself into a chair, rests his elbows on the table, and hides his face in his hands.)

Rebecca (coming quietly up behind him). Listen to me, John. If it were in your power to call Beata back—to you—to Rosmersholm—would you do it?

Rosmer. How can I tell what I would do or what I would not do! I have no thoughts for anything but the one thing which is irrevocable.

Rebecca. You ought to be beginning to live now, John. You were beginning. You had freed yourself completely on all sides. You were feeling so happy and so light-hearted

Rosmer. I know—that is true enough. And then comes this overwhelming blow.

Rebecca (standing behind him, with her arms on the back of his chair). How beautiful it was when we used to sit there downstairs in the dusk—and helped each other to plan our lives out afresh. You wanted to catch hold of actual life—the actual life of the day, as you used to say. You wanted to pass from house to house like a guest who brought emancipation with him—to win over men's thoughts and wills to your own—to fashion noble men all around you, in a wider and wider circle—noble men!

Rosmer. Noble men and happy men.

Rebecca. Yes, happy men.

Rosmer. Because it is happiness that gives the soul nobility, Rebecca.

Rebecca. Do you not think suffering too? The deepest suffering?

Rosmer. Yes, if one can win through it—conquer it—conquer it completely.

Rebecca. That is what you must do.

Rosmer (shaking his head sadly). I shall never conquer this completely. There will always be a doubt confronting me—a question. I shall never again be able to lose myself in the enjoyment of what makes life so wonderfully beautiful.

Rebecca (speaking over the back of his chair, softly). What do you mean, John?

Rosmer (looking up at her). Calm and happy innocence.

Rebecca (taking a step backwards). Of course. Innocence. (A short silence.)

Rosmer (resting his head on his hands with his elbows on the table, and looking straight in front of him). How ingeniously—how systematically—she must have put one thing together with another! First of all she begins to have a suspicion as to my orthodoxy. How on earth did she get that idea in her mind? Any way, she did; and the idea grew into a certainty. And then—then, of course, it was easy for her to think everything else possible. (Sits up in his chair and, runs his hands through his hair.) The wild fancies I am haunted with! I shall never get quit of them. I am certain of that—certain. They will always be starting up before me to remind me of the dead.

Rebecca. Like the White Horse of Rosmersholm.

Rosmer. Yes, like that. Rushing at me out of the dark—out of the silence.

Rebecca. And, because of this morbid fancy of yours, you are going to give up the hold you had just gained upon real life?

Rosmer. You are right, it seems hard—hard, Rebecca. But I have no power of choice in the matter. How do you think I could ever get the mastery over it?

Rebecca (standing behind his chair). By making new ties for yourself.

Rosmer (starts, and looks up). New ties?

Rebecca. Yes, new ties with the outside world. Live, work, do something! Do not sit here musing and brooding over insoluble conundrums.

Rosmer (getting up). New ties! (Walks across the room, turns at the door and comes back again.) A question occurs to my mind. Has it not occurred to you too, Rebecca?

Rebecca (catching her breath). Let me hear what it is.

Rosmer. What do you suppose will become of the tie between us, after to-day?

Rebecca. I think surely our friendship can endure, come what may.

Rosmer. Yes, but that is not exactly what I meant. I was thinking of what brought us together from the first, what links us so closely to one another—our common belief in the possibility of a man and a woman living together in chastity.

Rebecca. Yes, yes—what of it?

Rosmer. What I mean is—does not such a tie as that—such a tie as ours—seem to belong properly to a life lived in quiet, happy peacefulness?

Rebecca. Well?

Rosmer. But now I see stretching before me a life of strife and unrest and violent emotions. For I mean to live my life, Rebecca! I am not going to let myself be beaten to the ground by the dread of what may happen. I am not going to have my course of life prescribed for me, either by any living soul or by another.

Rebecca. No, no—do not! Be a free man in everything, John!

Rosmer. Do you understand what is in my Mind, then? Do you not know? Do you not see how I could best win my freedom from all these harrowing memories from the whole sad past?

Rebecca. Tell me!

Rosmer. By setting up, in opposition to them, a new and living reality.

Rebecca (feeling for the back of the chair). A living—? What do you mean?

Rosmer (coming closer to her). Rebecca—suppose I asked you now—will you be my second wife?

Rebecca (is speechless for a moment, then gives a cry of joy). Your wife! Yours—! I!

Rosmer. Yes—let us try what that will do. We two shall be one. There must no longer be any empty place left by the dead in this house.

Rebecca. I—in Beata's place—?

Rosmer. And then that chapter of my life will be closed—completely closed, never to be reopened.

Rebecca (in a low, trembling voice). Do you think so, John?

Rosmer. It must be so! It must! I cannot—I will not—go through life with a dead body on my back. Help me to throw it off, Rebecca; and then let us stifle all memories in our sense of freedom, in joy, in passion. You shall be to me the only wife I have ever had.

Rebecca (controlling herself). Never speak of this, again. I will never be your wife.

Rosmer. What! Never? Do you think, then, that you could not learn to love me? Is not our friendship already tinged with love?

Rebecca (stopping her ears, as if in fear). Don't speak like that, John! Don't say such things!

Rosmer (catching her by the arm). It is true! There is a growing possibility in the tie that is between us. I can see that you feel that, as well as I—do you not, Rebecca?

Rebecca (controlling herself completely). Listen. Let me tell you this—if you persist in this, I shall leave Rosmersholm.

Rosmer. Leave Rosmersholm! You! You cannot do that. It is impossible.

Rebecca. It is still more impossible for me to become your wife. Never, as long as I live, can I be that.

Rosmer (looks at her in surprise). You say "can"—and you say it so strangely. Why can you not?

Rebecca (taking both his hands in hers). Dear friend—for your own sake, as well as for mine, do not ask me why. (Lets go of his hands.) So, John. (Goes towards the door on the left.)

Rosmer. For the future the world will hold only one question for me—why?

Rebecca (turns and looks at him). In that case everything is at an end.

Rosmer. Between you and me?

Rebecca. Yes.

Rosmer. Things can never be at an end between us two. You shall never leave Rosmersholm.

Rebecca (with her hand on the door-handle). No, I dare say I shall not. But, all the same, if you question me again, it will mean the end of everything.

Rosmer. The end of everything, all the same? How—?

Rebecca. Because then I shall go the way Beata went. Now you know, John.

Rosmer. Rebecca—!

Rebecca (stops at the door and nods: slowly). Now you know. (Goes out.)

Rosmer (stares in bewilderment at the shut door, and says to himself): What can it mean?

ACT III

(SCENE. The sitting-room at Rosmersholm. The window and the hall-door are open. The morning sun is seen shining outside. REBECCA, dressed as in ACT I., is standing by the window, watering and arranging the flowers. Her work is lying on the armchair. MRS. HELSETH is going round the room with a feather brush, dusting the furniture.)

Rebecca (after a short pause). I wonder why Mr. Rosmer is so late in coming down to-day?

Mrs. Helseth. Oh, he is often as late as this, miss. He is sure to be down directly.

Rebecca. Have you seen anything of him?

Mrs. Helseth. No, miss, except that as I took his coffee into his study he went into his bedroom to finish dressing.

Rebecca. The reason I ask is that he was not very well yesterday.

Mrs. Helseth. No, he did not look well. It made me wonder whether something had gone amiss between him and his brother-in-law.

Rebecca. What do you suppose could go amiss between them?

Mrs. Helseth. I can't say, miss. Perhaps it was that fellow Mortensgaard set them at loggerheads.

Rebecca. It is quite possible. Do you know anything of this Peter Mortensgaard?

Mrs. Helseth. Not I! How could you think so, miss—a man like that!

Rebecca. Because of that horrid paper he edits, you mean?

Mrs. Helseth. Not only because of that, miss. I suppose you have heard that a certain married woman, whose husband had deserted her, had a child by him?

Rebecca. I have heard it; but of course that was long before I came here.

Mrs. Helseth. Bless me, yes—he was quite a young man then. But she might have had more sense than he had. He wanted to marry her, too, but that could not be done; and so he had to pay heavily for it. But since then—my word!—Mortensgaard has risen in the world. There are lots of people who run after him now.

Rebecca. I believe most of the poor people turn to him first when they are in any trouble.

Mrs. Helseth. Oh, not only the poor people, miss—

Rebecca (glancing at her unobserved). Indeed?

Mrs. Helseth (standing at the sofa, dusting vigorously). People you would least expect, sometimes, miss.

Rebecca (arranging the flowers). Yes, but that is only an idea of yours, Mrs. Helseth. You cannot know that for certain.

Mrs. Helseth. You think I don't know anything about that for certain, do you, miss? Indeed I do. Because—if I must let out the secret at last—I carried a letter to Mortensgaard myself once.

Rebecca (turns round). No—did you!

Mrs. Helseth. Yes, that I did. And that letter, let me tell you, was written here—at Rosmersholm.

Rebecca. Really, Mrs. Helseth?

Mrs. Helseth. I give you my word it was, miss. And it was written on good note-paper—and sealed with beautiful red sealing-wax.

Rebecca. And you were entrusted with the delivery of it? Dear Mrs. Helseth, it is not very difficult to guess whom it was from.

Mrs. Helseth. Who, then?

Rebecca. Naturally, it was something that poor Mrs. Rosmer in her invalid state—

Mrs. Helseth. Well, you have mentioned her name, miss—not I.

Rebecca. But what was in the letter?—No, of course, you cannot know that.

Mrs. Helseth. Hm!—it is just possible I may know, all the same.

Rebecca. Did she tell you what she was writing about, then?

Mrs. Helseth. No, she did not do that. But when Mortensgaard had read it, he set to work and cross-questioned me, so that I got a very good idea of what was in it.

Rebecca. What do you think was in it, then? Oh, dear, good Mrs. Helseth, do tell me!

Mrs. Helseth. Certainly not, miss. Not for worlds.

Rebecca. Oh, you can tell me. You and I are such friends, you know.

Mrs. Helseth. Heaven forbid I should tell you anything about that, miss. I shall not tell you anything, except that it was some dreadful idea that they had gone and put into my poor sick mistress's head.

Rebecca. Who had put it into her head?

Mrs. Helseth. Wicked people, miss. Wicked people.

Rebecca. Wicked—?

Mrs. Helseth. Yes, I say it again—very wicked people, they must have been.

Rebecca. And what do you think it could be?

Mrs. Helseth. Oh, I know what I think—but, please Heaven, I'll keep my mouth shut. At the same time, there is a certain lady in the town—hm!

Rebecca. I can see you mean Mrs. Kroll.

Mrs. Helseth. Yes, she is a queer one, she is. She has always been very much on the high horse with me. And she has never looked with any friendly eye on you, either, miss.

Rebecca. Do you think Mrs. Rosmer was quite in her right mind when she wrote that letter to Mortensgaard?

Mrs. Helseth. It is so difficult to tell, miss. I certainly don't think she was quite out of her mind.

Rebecca. But you know she seemed to go quite distracted when she learnt that she would never be able to have a child. That was when her madness first showed itself.

Mrs. Helseth. Yes, that had a terrible effect on her, poor lady.

Rebecca (taking up her work, and sitting down on a chair by the window). But, in other respects, do you not think that was really a good thing for Mr. Rosmer, Mrs. Helseth?

Mrs. Helseth. What, miss?

Rebecca. That there were no children?

Mrs. Helseth. Hm!—I really do not know what to say to that.

Rebecca. Believe me, it was best for him. Mr. Rosmer was never meant to be surrounded by crying children.

Mrs. Helseth. Little children do not cry at Rosmersholm, Miss West.

Rebecca (looking at her). Not cry?

Mrs. Helseth. No. In this house, little children have never been known to cry, as long as any one can remember.

Rebecca. That is very strange.

Mrs. Helseth. Yes, isn't it, miss? But it runs in the family. And there is another thing that is just as strange; when they grow up they never laugh—never laugh, all their lives.

Rebecca. But that would be extraordinary

Mrs. Helseth. Have you ever once heard or seen Mr. Rosmer laugh, miss?

Rebecca. No—now that I think of it, I almost believe you are right. But I fancy most of the folk hereabouts laugh very little.

Mrs. Helseth. That is quite true. People say it began at Rosmersholm, and I expect it spread like a sort of infection.

Rebecca. You are a sagacious woman, Mrs. Helseth!

Mrs. Helseth. Oh, you mustn't sit there and make game of me, miss. (Listens.) Hush, hush—Mr. Rosmer is coming down. He doesn't like to see brooms about. (Goes out by the door on the right. ROSMER, with his stick and hat in his hand, comes in from the lobby.)

Rosmer. Good-morning, Rebecca.

Rebecca. Good-morning, dear. (She goes on working for a little while in silence.) Are you going out?

Rosmer. Yes.

Rebecca. It is such a lovely day.

Rosmer. You did not come up to see me this morning.

Rebecca. No—I didn't. Not to-day.

Rosmer. Don't you mean to do so in future, either? Rebecca. I cannot say yet, dear.

Rosmer. Has anything come for me?

Rebecca. The "County News" has come.

Rosmer. The "County News"!

Rebecca. There it is, on the table.

Rosmer (putting down his hat and stick). Is there anything—?

Rebecca. Yes.

Rosmer. And you did not send it up to me

Rebecca. You will read it quite soon enough.

Rosmer. Well, let us see. (Takes up the paper and stands by the table reading it.) What!—"cannot pronounce too emphatic a warning against unprincipled deserters." (Looks at her.) They call me a deserter, Rebecca.

Rebecca. They mention no names at all.

Rosmer. It comes to the same thing. (Goes on reading.) "Secret traitors to the good cause."—"Judas-like creatures, who shamelessly confess their apostasy as soon as they think the most opportune and most profitable moment has arrived."—"A reckless outrage on the fair fame of honoured ancestors"—"in the expectation that those who are enjoying a brief spell of authority will not disappoint them of a suitable reward." (Lays the paper down on the table.) And they write that of me—these men who have known me so long and so intimately—write a thing that they do not even believe themselves! They know there is not a single word of truth in it—and yet they write it.

Rebecca. There is more of it yet.

Rosmer (taking up the paper again). "Make some allowance for inexperience and want of judgment"—"a pernicious influence which, very possibly, has extended even to matters which for the present we will refrain from publicly discussing or condemning." (Looks at her.) What does that mean?

Rebecca. That is a hit at me, obviously.

Rosmer (laying down the paper). Rebecca, this is the conduct of dishonourable men.

Rebecca. Yes, it seems to me they have no right to talk about Mortensgaard.

Rosmer (walking up and down the room). They must be saved from this sort of thing. All the good that is in men is destroyed, if it is allowed to go on. But it shall not be so! How happy—how happy I should feel if I could succeed in bringing a little light into all this murky ugliness.

Rebecca (getting up). I am sure of it. There is something great, something splendid, for you to live for!

Rosmer. Just think of it—if I could wake them to a real knowledge of themselves—bring them to be angry with and ashamed of themselves—induce them to be at one with each other in toleration, in love, Rebecca!

Rebecca. Yes! Give yourself up entirely to that task, and you will see that you will succeed.

Rosmer. I think it might be done. What happiness it would be to live one's life, then! No more hateful strife—only emulation; every eye fixed on the same goal; every man's will, every man's thoughts moving forward-upward—each in its own inevitable path Happiness for all—and through the efforts of all! (Looks out of the window as he speaks, then gives a start and says gloomily:) Ah! not through me.

Rebecca. Not—not through you?

Rosmer. Nor for me, either.

Rebecca. Oh, John, have no such doubts.

Rosmer. Happiness, dear Rebecca, means first and foremost the calm, joyous sense of innocence.

Rebecca (staring in front of her). Ah, innocence—

Rosmer. You need fear nothing on that score. But I—

Rebecca. You least of all men!

Rosmer (pointing out of the window). The mill-race.

Rebecca. Oh, John!—(MRS. HELSETH looks in in through the door on the left.)

Mrs. Helseth. Miss West!

Rebecca. Presently, presently. Not now.

Mrs. Helseth. Just a word, miss! (REBECCA goes to the door. MRS. HELSETH tells her something, and they whisper together for a moment; then MRS. HELSETH nods and goes away.)

Rosmer (uneasily). Was it anything for me?

Rebecca. No, only something about the housekeeping. You ought to go out into the open air now, John dear. You should go for a good long walk.

Rosmer (taking up his hat). Yes, come along; we will go together.

Rebecca. No, dear, I can't just now. You must go by yourself. But shake off all these gloomy thoughts—promise me that!

Rosmer. I shall never be able to shake them quite off, I am afraid.

Rebecca. Oh, but how can you let such groundless fancies take such a hold on you!

Rosmer. Unfortunately they are not so groundless as you think, dear. I have lain, thinking them over, all night. Perhaps Beata saw things truly after all.

Rebecca. In what way do you mean?

Rosmer. Saw things truly when she believed I loved you, Rebecca.

Rebecca. Truly in THAT respect?

Rosmer (laying his hat down on the table). This is the question I have been wrestling with—whether we two have deluded ourselves the whole time, when we have been calling the tie between us merely friendship.

Rebecca. Do you mean, then, that the right name for it would have been—?

Rosmer. Love. Yes, dear, that is what I mean. Even while Beata was alive, it was you that I gave all my thoughts to. It was you alone I yearned for. It was with you that I experienced peaceful, joyful, passionless happiness. When we consider it rightly, Rebecca, our life together began like the sweet, mysterious love of two children for one another—free from desire or any thought of anything more. Did you not feel it in that way too? Tell me.

Rebecca (struggling with herself). Oh, I do not know what to answer.

Rosmer. And it was this life of intimacy, with one another and for one another, that we took to be friendship. No, dear—the tie between us has been a spiritual marriage—perhaps from the very first day. That is why I am guilty. I had no right to it—no right to it for Beata's sake.

Rebecca. No right to a happy life? Do you believe that, John?

Rosmer. She looked at the relations between us through the eyes of HER love—judged them after the nature of HER love. And it was only natural. She could not have judged them otherwise than she did.

Rebecca. But how can you so accuse yourself for Beata's delusions?

Rosmer. It was for love of me—in her own way that—she threw herself into the mill-race. That fact is certain, Rebecca. I can never get beyond that.

Rebecca. Oh, do not think of anything else but the great, splendid task that you are going to devote your life to!

Rosmer (shaking his head). It can never be carried through. Not by me. Not after what I know now.

Rebecca. Why not by you?

Rosmer. Because no cause can ever triumph which has its beginnings in guilt.

Rebecca (impetuously). Oh, these are nothing but prejudices you have inherited—these doubts, these fears, these scruples! You have a legend here that your dead return to haunt you in the form of white horses. This seems to me to be something of that sort.

Rosmer. Be that as it may, what difference does it make if I cannot shake it off? Believe me, Rebecca, it is as I say—any cause which is to win a lasting victory must be championed by a man who is joyous and innocent.

Rebecca. But is joy so absolutely indispensable to you, John?

Rosmer. Joy? Yes, indeed it is.

Rebecca. To you, who never laugh?

Rosmer. Yes, in spite of that. Believe me, I have a great capacity for joy.

Rebecca. Now you really must go out, dear—for a long walk—a really long one, do you hear? There is your hat, and there is your stick.

Rosmer (taking them from her). Thank you. And you won't come too?

Rebecca. No, no, I can't come now.

Rosmer. Very well. You are none the less always with me now. (Goes out by the entrance hall. After a moment REBECCA peeps out from behind the door which he has left open. Then she goes to the door on the right, which she opens.)

Rebecca (in a whisper). Now, Mrs. Helseth. You can let him come in now. (Crosses to the window. A moment later, KROLL comes in from the right. He bows to her silently and formally and keeps his hat in his hand.)

Kroll. Has he gone, then?

Rebecca. Yes.

Kroll. Does he generally stay out long?

Rebecca. Yes. But to-day he is in a very uncertain mood—so, if you do not want to meet him—

Kroll. Certainly not. It is you I wish to speak to—and quite alone.

Rebecca. Then we had better make the best of our time. Please sit down. (She sits down in an easy-chair by the window. KROLL takes a chair beside her.)

Kroll. Miss West, you can scarcely have any idea how deeply pained and unhappy I am over this revolution that has taken place in John Rosmer's ideas.

Rebecca. We were prepared for that being so—at first.

Kroll. Only at first?

Rosmer. Mr. Rosmer hoped confidently that sooner or later you would take your place beside him.

Kroll. I?

Rebecca. You and all his other friends.

Kroll. That should convince you how feeble his judgment is on any matter concerning his fellow-creatures and the affairs of real life.

Rebecca. In any case, now that he feels the absolute necessity of cutting himself free on all sides—

Kroll. Yes; but, let me tell you, that is exactly what I do not believe.

Rebecca. What do you believe, then?

Kroll. I believe it is you that are at the bottom of the whole thing.

Rebecca. Your wife put that into your head, Mr. Kroll.

Kroll. It does not matter who put it into my head. The point is this, that I feel grave doubts—exceedingly grave doubts—when I recall and think over the whole of your behaviour since you came here.

Rebecca (looking at him). I have a notion that there was a time when you had an exceedingly strong BELIEF in me, dear Mr. Kroll—I might almost say, a warm belief.

Kroll (in a subdued voice). I believe you could bewitch any one—if you set yourself to do it.

Rebecca. And you say I set myself to do it!

Kroll. Yes, you did. I am no longer such a simpleton as to suppose that sentiment entered into your little game at all. You simply wanted to secure yourself admission to Rosmersholm—to establish yourself here. That was what I was to help you to. I see it now.

Rebecca. Then you have completely forgotten that it was Beata that begged and entreated me to come and live here.

Kroll. Yes, because you had bewitched her too. Are you going to pretend that friendship is the name for what she came to feel towards you? It was idolatry—

adoration. It degenerated into a—what shall I call, it?—a sort of desperate passion. Yes, that is just the word for it.

Rebecca. Have the goodness to remember the condition your sister was in. As far as I am concerned I do not think I can be said to be particularly emotional in any way.

Kroll. No, you certainly are not. But that makes you all the more dangerous to those whom you wish to get into your power. It comes easy to you to act with deliberation and careful calculation, just because you have a cold heart.

Rebecca. Cold? Are you so sure of that?

Kroll. I am certain of it now. Otherwise you could not have pursued your object here so unswervingly, year after year. Yes, yes—you have gained what you wanted. You have got him and everything else here into your power. But, to carry out your schemes, you have not scrupled to make him unhappy.

Rebecca. That is not true. It is not I; it is you yourself that have made him unhappy.

Kroll. I!

Rebecca. Yes, by leading him to imagine that he was responsible for the terrible end that overtook Beata.

Kroll. Did that affect him so deeply, then?

Rebecca. Of course. A man of such gentle disposition as he—

Kroll. I imagined that one of your so-called "emancipated" men would know how to overcome any scruples. But there it is! Oh, yes—as a matter of fact it turned out just as I expected. The descendant of the men who are looking at us from these walls need not think he can break loose from what has been handed down as an inviolable inheritance from generation to generation.

Rebecca (looking thoughtfully in front of her). John Rosmer's nature is deeply rooted in his ancestors. That is certainly very true.

Kroll. Yes, and you ought to have taken that into consideration, if you had had any sympathy for him. But I dare say you were incapable of that sort of consideration. Your starting-point is so very widely-removed from his, you see.

Rebecca. What do you mean by my starting-point?

Kroll. I mean the starting-point of origin—of parentage, Miss West.

Rebecca. I see. Yes, it is quite true that my origin is very humble. But nevertheless—

Kroll. I am not alluding to rank or position. I am thinking of the moral aspect of your origin.

Rebecca. Of my origin? In what respect?

Kroll. In respect of your birth generally.

Rebecca. What are you saying!

Kroll. I am only saying it because it explains the whole of your conduct.

Rebecca. I do not understand. Be so good as to tell me exactly what you mean.

Kroll. I really thought you did not need telling. Otherwise it would seem a very strange thing that you let yourself be adopted by Dr. West.

Rebecca (getting up). Oh, that is it! Now I understand.

Kroll. And took his name. Your mother's name was Gamvik.

Rebecca (crossing the room). My father's name was Gamvik, Mr. Kroll.

Kroll. Your mother's occupation must, of course, have brought her continually into contact with the district physician.

Rebecca. You are quite right.

Kroll. And then he takes you to live with him, immediately upon your mother's death. He treats you harshly, and yet you stay with him. You know that he will not leave you a single penny—as a matter of fact you only got a box of books—and yet you endure living with him, put up with his behaviour, and nurse him to the end.

Rebecca (comes to the table and looks at him scornfully). And my doing all that makes it clear to you that there was something immoral—something criminal about my birth!

Kroll. What you did for him, I attributed to an unconscious filial instinct. And, as far as the rest of it goes, I consider that the whole of your conduct has been the outcome of your origin.

Rebecca (hotly). But there is not a single word of truth in what you say! And I can prove it! Dr. West had not come to Finmark when I was born.

Kroll. Excuse me, Miss West. He went there a year before you were born. I have ascertained that.

Rebecca. You are mistaken, I tell you! You are absolutely mistaken!

Kroll. You said here, the day before yesterday, that you were twenty-nine—going on for thirty.

Rebecca. Really? Did I say that?

Kroll. Yes, you did. And from that I can calculate—

Rebecca. Stop! That will not help you to calculate. For, I may as well tell you at once, I am a year older than I give myself out to be.

Kroll (smiling incredulously). Really? That is something new. How is that?

Rebecca. When I had passed my twenty-fifth birthday, I thought I was getting altogether too old for an unmarried girl, so I resolved to tell a lie and take a year off my age.

Kroll. You—an emancipated woman—cherishing prejudices as to the marriageable age!

Rebecca. I know it was a silly thing to do—and ridiculous, too. But every one has some prejudice or another that they cannot get quite rid of. We are like that.

Kroll. Maybe. But my calculation may be quite correct, all the same; because Dr. West was up in Finmark for a flying visit the year before he was appointed.

Rebecca (impetuously). That is not true

Kroll. Isn't it?

Rebecca. No. My mother never mentioned it.

Kroll. Didn't she, really!

Rebecca. No, never. Nor Dr. West, either. Never a word of it.

Kroll. Might that not be because they both had good reason to jump over a year?—@just as you have done yourself, Miss West? Perhaps it is a family failing.

Rebecca (walking about, wringing her hands). It is impossible. It is only something you want to make me believe. Nothing in the world will make me believe it. It cannot be true! Nothing in the world—

Kroll (getting up). But, my dear Miss West, why in Heaven's name do you take it in this way? You quite alarm me! What am I to believe and think?

Rebecca. Nothing. Neither believe nor think anything.

Kroll. Then you really must give me some explanation of your taking this matter—this possibility—so much to heart.

Rebecca (controlling herself). It is quite obvious, I should think, Mr. Kroll. I have no desire for people here to think me an illegitimate child.

Kroll. Quite so. Well, well, let us be content with your explanation, for the present. But you see that is another point on which you have cherished a certain prejudice.

Rebecca. Yes, that is quite true.

Kroll. And it seems to me that very much the same applies to most of this "emancipation" of yours, as you call it. Your reading has introduced you to a hotch-potch of new ideas and opinions; you have made a certain acquaintance with researches that are going on in various directions—researches that seem to you to upset a good many ideas that people have hitherto considered incontrovertible and unassailable. But all this has never gone any further than knowledge in your case, Miss West—a mere matter of the intellect. It has not got into your blood.

Rebecca (thoughtfully). Perhaps you are right.

Kroll. Yes, only test yourself, and you will see! And if it is true in your case, it is easy to recognise how true it must be in John Rosmer's. Of course it is madness, pure and simple. He will be running headlong to his ruin if he persists in coming openly forward and proclaiming himself an apostate! Just think of it—he, with his shy disposition! Think of HIM disowned—hounded out of the circle to which he has always belonged—exposed to the uncompromising attacks of all the best people in the place. Nothing would ever make him the man to endure that.

Rebecca. He MUST endure it! It is too late now for him to draw back.

Kroll. Not a bit too late—not by any means too late. What has happened can be hushed up—or at any rate can be explained away as a purely temporary, though regrettable, aberration. But—there is one step that it is absolutely essential he should take.

Rebecca. And that is?

Kroll. You must get him to legalise his position, Miss West.

Rebecca. The position in which he stands to me?

Kroll. Yes. You must see that you get him to do that.

Rebecca. Then you can't rid yourself of the conviction that the relations between us need "legalising," as you say?

Kroll. I do not wish to go any more precisely into the question. But I certainly have observed that the conditions under which it always seems easiest for people to abandon all their so-called prejudices are when—ahem!

Rebecca. When it is a question of the relations between a man and a woman, I suppose you mean?

Kroll. Yes—to speak candidly—that is what I mean.

Rebecca (walks across the room and looks out of the window). I was on the point of saying that I wish you had been right, Mr. Kroll.

Kroll. What do you mean by that? You say it so strangely!

Rebecca. Oh, nothing! Do not let us talk any more about it. Ah, there he is!

Kroll. Already! I will go, then.

Rebecca (turning to him). No—stay here, and you will hear something.

Kroll. Not now. I do not think I could bear to see him.

Rebecca. I beg you to stay. Please do, or you will regret it later. It is the last time

I shall ever ask you to do anything.

Kroll (looks at her in surprise, and lays his hat down). Very well, Miss West. It shall be as you wish. (A short pause. Then ROSMER comes in from the hall.)

Rosmer (stops at the door, as he sees KROLL). What! you here?

Rebecca. He wanted to avoid meeting you, John.

Kroll (involuntarily). "John?"

Rebecca. Yes, Mr. Kroll. John and I call each other by our Christian names. That is a natural consequence of the relations between us.

Kroll. Was that what I was to hear if I stayed?

Rebecca. Yes, that and something else.

Rosmer (coming into the room). What is the object of your visit here to-day?

Kroll. I wanted to make one more effort to stop you, and win you back.

Rosmer (pointing to the newspaper). After that?

Kroll. I did not write it.

Rosmer. Did you take any steps to prevent its appearing?

Kroll. That would have been acting unjustifiably towards the cause I serve. And, besides that, I had no power to prevent it.

Rebecca (tears the newspaper into pieces, which she crumples up and throws into the back of the stove). There! Now it is out of sight; let it be out of mind too. Because there will be no more of that sort of thing, John.

Kroll. Indeed, I wish you could ensure that.

Rebecca. Come, and let us sit down, dear—all three of us. Then I will tell you all about it.

Rosmer (sitting down involuntarily). What has come over you, Rebecca? You are so unnaturally calm—What is it?

Rebecca. The calmness of determination. (Sits down.) Please sit down too, Mr. Kroll. (He takes a seat on the couch.)

Rosmer. Determination, you say. Determination to do what?

Rebecca. I want to give you back what you need in order to live your life. You shall have your happy innocence back, dear friend.

Rosmer. But what do you mean?

Rebecca. I will just tell you what happened. That is all that is necessary.

Rosmer. Well?

Rebecca. When I came down here from Finmark with Dr. West, it seemed to me that a new, great, wide world was opened to me. Dr. West had given me an erratic sort of education—had taught me all the odds and ends that I knew about life then. (Has an evident struggle with herself, and speaks in barely audible tones.) And then—

Kroll. And then?

Rosmer. But, Rebecca—I know all this.

Rebecca (collecting herself). Yes—that is true enough. You know it only too well.

Kroll (looking fixedly at her). Perhaps it would be better if I left you.

Rebecca. No, stay where you are, dear Mr. Kroll. (To ROSMER.) Well, this was how it was. I wanted to play my part in the new day that was dawning—to have a share in all the new ideas. Mr. Kroll told me one day that Ulrik Brendel had had a great influence over you once, when you were a boy. I thought it might be possible for me to resume that influence here.

Rosmer. Did you come here with a covert design?

Rebecca. What I wanted was that we two should go forward together on the road towards freedom—always forward, and further forward! But there was that gloomy, insurmountable barrier between you and a full, complete emancipation.

Rosmer. What barrier do you mean?

Rebecca. I mean, John, that you could never have attained freedom except in the full glory of the sunshine. And, instead of that, here you were—ailing and languishing in the gloom of such a marriage as yours.

Rosmer. You have never spoken to me of my marriage in that way, before to-day.

Rebecca. No, I did not dare, for fear of frightening you.

Kroll (nodding to ROSMER). You hear that!

Rebecca (resuming). But I saw quite well where your salvation lay—your only salvation. And so I acted.

Rosmer. How do you mean—you acted?

Kroll. Do you mean that?

Rebecca. Yes, John. (Gets up.) No, do not get up. Nor you either, Mr. Kroll. But we must let in the daylight now. It was not you, John. You are innocent. It was I that lured—that ended by luring—Beata into the tortuous path—

Rosmer (springing up). Rebecca!

Kroll (getting up). Into the tortuous path!

Rebecca. Into the path that—led to the mill-race. Now you know it, both of you.

Rosmer (as if stunned). But I do not understand—What is she standing there saying? I do not understand a word—

Kroll. Yes, yes. I begin to understand.

Rosmer. But what did you do? What did you find to tell her? Because there was nothing—absolutely nothing!

Rebecca. She got to know that you were determined to emancipate yourself from all your old prejudices.

Rosmer. Yes, but at that time I had come to no decision.

Rebecca. I knew that you soon would come to one.

Kroll (nodding to ROSMER). Aha!

Rosmer. Well—and what more? I want to know everything now.

Rebecca. Some time afterwards, I begged and implored her to let me leave Rosmersholm.

Rosmer. Why did you want to leave here—then?

Rebecca. I did not want to. I wanted to remain where I was. But I told her that it would be best for us all if I went away in time. I let her infer that if I remained here any longer I could not tell what-what-might happen.

Rosmer. That is what you said and did, then?

Rebecca. Yes, John.

Rosmer. That is what you referred to when you said that you "acted"?

Rebecca (in a broken voice). Yes, that was it.

Rosmer (after a pause). Have you confessed everything now, Rebecca?

Rebecca. Yes.

Kroll. Not everything.

Rebecca (looking at him in terror). What else can there be?

Kroll. Did you not eventually lead Beata to believe that it was necessary—not merely that it should be best—but that it was necessary, both for your own sake and for John's, that you should go away somewhere else as soon as possible?—Well?

Rebecca (speaking low and indistinctly). Perhaps I did say something of the sort.

Rosmer (sinking into a chair by the window). And she, poor sick creature, believed in this tissue of lies and deceit! Believed in it so completely—so absolutely! (Looks up at REBECCA.) And she never came to me about it—never said a word! Ah, Rebecca—I see it in your face—YOU dissuaded her from doing so.

Rebecca. You know she had taken it into her head that she, a childless wife, had no right to be here. And so she persuaded herself that her duty to you was to give place to another.

Rosmer. And you—you did nothing to rid her mind of such an idea?

Rebecca. No.

Kroll. Perhaps you encouraged her in the idea? Answer! Did you not do so?

Rebecca. That was how she understood me, I believe.

Rosmer. Yes, yes—and she bowed to your will in everything. And so she gave place. (Springs up.) How could you—how could you go on with this terrible tragedy!

Rebecca. I thought there were two lives here to choose between, John.

Kroll (severely and with authority). You had no right to make any such choice.

Rebecca (impetuously). Surely you do not think I acted with cold and calculating composure! I am a different woman now, when I am telling you this, from what I was then. And I believe two different kinds of will can exist at the same time in one person. I wanted Beata away—in one way or the other; but I never thought it would happen, all the same. At every step I ventured and risked, I seemed to hear a voice in me crying: "No further! Not a step further!" And yet, at the same time, I COULD not stop. I HAD to venture a little bit further—just one step. And then another—and always another—and at last it happened. That is how such things go of themselves. (A short silence.)

Rosmer (to REBECCA). And how do you think it will go with YOU in the future?—after this?

Rebecca. Things must go with me as they can. It is of very little consequence.

Kroll. Not a word suggestive of remorse! Perhaps you feel none?

Rebecca (dismissing his remark coldly). Excuse me, Mr. Kroll, that is a matter that is no concern of any one else's. That is an account I must settle with myself.

Kroll (to ROSMER). And this is the woman you have been living under the same roof with—in relations of the completest confidence. (Looks up at the portraits on the walls.) If only those that are gone could look down now!

Rosmer. Are you going into the town?

Kroll (taking up his hat). Yes. The sooner the better.

Rosmer (taking his hat also). Then I will go with you.

Kroll. You will! Ah, I thought we had not quite lost you.

Rosmer. Come, then, Kroll. Come! (They both go out into the hall without looking at REBECCA. After a minute REBECCA goes cautiously to the window and peeps out between the flowers.)

Rebecca (speaking to herself, half aloud). Not over the bridge to-day either. He is going round. Never over the millrace—never. (Comes away from the window.) As I thought! (She goes over to the bell, and rings it. Soon afterwards MRS. HELSETH comes in from the right.)

Mrs. Helseth. What is it, miss?

Rebecca. Mrs. Helseth, will you be so good as to fetch my travelling trunk down from the loft?

Mrs. Helseth. Your trunk?

Rebecca. Yes, the brown hair-trunk, you know.

Mrs. Helseth. Certainly, miss. But, bless my soul, are you going away on a journey, miss?

Rebecca. Yes—I am going away on a journey, Mrs. Helseth.

Mrs. Helseth. And immediately!

Rebecca. As soon as I have packed.

Mrs. Helseth. I never heard of such a thing! But you are coming back again soon, I suppose, miss?

Rebecca. I am never coming back again.

Mrs. Helseth. Never! But, my goodness, what is to become of us at Rosmersholm if Miss West is not here any longer? Just as everything was making poor Mr. Rosmer so happy and comfortable!

Rebecca. Yes, but to-day I have had a fright, Mrs. Helseth.

Mrs. Helseth. A fright! Good heavens-how?

Rebecca. I fancy I have had a glimpse of the White Horse.

Mrs. Helseth. Of the White Horse! In broad daylight!

Rebecca. Ah! they are out both early and late, the White Horses of Rosmersholm. (Crosses the room.) Well—we were speaking of my trunk, Mrs. Helseth.

Mrs. Helseth. Yes, miss. Your trunk.

(They both go out to the right.)

ACT IV

(SCENE.—The same room in the late evening. The lamp, with a shade on it, is burning on the table. REBECCA is standing by the table, packing some small articles in a travelling-bag. Her cloak, hat, and the white crochetted shawl are hanging on the back of the couch. MRS. HELSETH comes in from the right.)

Mrs. Helseth (speaking in low tones and with a reserved manner). Yes, all your things have been taken down, miss. They are in the kitchen passage.

Rebecca. Thank you. You have ordered the carriage?

Mrs. Helseth. Yes, miss. The coachman wants to know what time he shall bring it round.

Rebecca. I think at about eleven o'clock. The boat goes at midnight.

Mrs. Helseth (with a little hesitation). But what about Mr. Rosmer? Suppose he is not back by that time?

Rebecca. I shall start, all the same. If I should not see him, you can tell him I will write to him—a long letter, say that.

Mrs. Helseth. Yes, I dare say it will be all right to write. But, poor dear, I really think that you ought to try and have a talk with him once more.

Rebecca. Perhaps I ought—Or perhaps not, after all.

Mrs. Helseth. Dear, dear! I never thought I should, live to see such a thing as this!

Rebecca. What did you think, then, Mrs. Helseth?

Mrs. Helseth. To tell the truth, miss, I thought Mr. Rosmer was an honester man than that.

Rebecca. Honester?

Mrs. Helseth. Yes, miss, that is the truth.

Rebecca. But, my dear Mrs. Helseth, what do you mean by that?

Mrs. Helseth. I mean what is true and right, miss. He should not get out of it in this way—that he shouldn't.

Rebecca (looking at her). Now look here, Mrs. Helseth. Tell me, honestly and frankly, why you think I am going away.

Mrs. Helseth. Good Lord, miss—because it is necessary, I suppose. Well, well!—Still, I certainly do not think Mr. Rosmer has behaved well. There was some excuse in Mortensgaard's case, because the woman's husband was still alive; so that it was impossible for them to marry, however much they wished it. But Mr. Rosmer, he could—ahem!

Rebecca (with a faint smile). Is it possible that you could think such things about me and Mr. Rosmer?

Mrs. Helseth. Not for a moment—until to-day, I mean.

Rebecca. But why to-day?

Mrs. Helseth. Well, after all the horrible things they tell me one may see in the papers about Mr. Rosmer—

Rebecca. Ah!

Mrs. Helseth. What I mean is this—if a man can go over to Mortensgaard's religion, you may believe him capable of anything. And that's the truth.

Rebecca. Yes, very likely. But about me? What have you got to say about me?

Mrs. Helseth. Well, I am sure, miss—I do not think you are so greatly to be blamed. It is not always so easy for a lone woman to resist, I dare say. We are all human after all, Miss West.

Rebecca. That is very true, Mrs. Helseth. We are all human, after all.—What are you listening to?

Mrs. Helseth (in a low voice). Good Lord!—I believe that is him coming now.

Rebecca (with a start). In spite of everything, then—! (Speaks with determination.) Very well. So be it. (ROSMER comes in from the hall. He sees the luggage, and turns to REBECCA.)

Rosmer. What does this mean?

Rebecca. I am going away.

Rosmer. At once?

Rebecca. Yes. (To MRS. HELSETH.) Eleven o'clock, then.

Mrs. Helseth. Very well, miss. (Goes out to the right.)

Rosmer (after a short pause). Where are you going, Rebecca?

Rebecca. I am taking the boat for the north.

Rosmer. North? What are you going there for?

Rebecca. It is where I came from.

Rosmer. But you have no more ties there now.

Rebecca. I have none here, either.

Rosmer. What do you propose to do?

Rebecca. I do not know. I only want to make an end of it.

Rosmer. Make an end of what?

Rebecca. Rosmersholm has broken me.

Rosmer (more attentively). What is that?

Rebecca. Broken me utterly. I had a will of my own, and some courage, when I came here. Now I am crushed under the law of strangers. I do not think I shall have the courage to begin anything else in the world after this.

Rosmer. Why not? What do you mean by being crushed under a law—?

Rebecca. Dear friend, do not let us talk about that now—Tell me what passed between you and Mr. Kroll.

Rosmer. We have made our peace.

Rebecca. Quite so. So it came to that.

Rosmer. He got together all our old circle of friends at his house. They convinced me that the work of ennobling men's souls was not in my line at all. Besides, it is such a hopeless task, any way. I shall let it alone.

Rebecca. Well, perhaps it is better so.

Rosmer. Do you say THAT now? Is that what your opinion is now?

Rebecca. I have come to that opinion—in the last day or two.

Rosmer. You are lying, Rebecca.

Rebecca. Lying—?

Rosmer. Yes, lying. You have never believed in me. You have never believed me to be the man to lead the cause to victory.

Rebecca. I have believed that we two together would be equal to it.

Rosmer. That is not true. You have believed that you could accomplish something big in life yourself—that you could use me to further your plans—that I might be useful to you in the pursuit of your object. That is what you have believed.

Rebecca. Listen to me, John

Rosmer (sitting down wearily on the couch). Oh, let me be! I see the whole thing clearly now. I have been like a glove in your hands.

Rebecca. Listen to me, John. Let us talk this thing over. It will be for the last time. (Sits down in a chair by the couch.) I had intended to write to you about it all—when I had gone back north. But it is much better that you should hear it at once.

Rosmer. Have you something more to tell, then?

Rebecca. The most important part of it all.

Rosmer. What do you mean?

Rebecca. Something that you have never suspected. Something that puts all the rest in its true light.

Rosmer (shaking his head). I do not understand, at all.

Rebecca. It is quite true that at one time I did play my cards so as to secure admission to Rosmersholm. My idea was that I should succeed in doing well for myself here—either in one way or in another, you understand.

Rosmer. Well, you succeeded in carrying your scheme through, too.

Rebecca. I believe I could have carried anything through—at that time. For then I still had the courage of a free will. I had no one else to consider, nothing to turn me from my path. But then began what has broken down my will and filled the whole of my life with dread and wretchedness.

Rosmer. What—began? Speak so that I can understand you.

Rebecca. There came over me—a wild, uncontrollable passion—Oh, John—!

Rosmer. Passion? You—! For what?

Rebecca. For you.

Rosmer (getting up). What does this mean!

Rebecca (preventing him). Sit still, dear. I will tell you more about it.

Rosmer. And you mean to say—that you have loved me—in that way!

Rebecca. I thought I might call it loving you—then. I thought it was love. But it was not. It was what I have said—a wild, uncontrollable passion.

Rosmer (speaking with difficulty). Rebecca—is it really you—you—who are sitting here telling me this?

Rebecca. Yes, indeed it is, John.

Rosmer. Then it was as the outcome of this—and under the influence of this—that you "acted," as you called it.

Rebecca. It swept over me like a storm over the sea—like one of the storms we have in winter in the north. They catch you up and rush you along with them, you know, until their fury is expended. There is no withstanding them.

Rosmer. So it swept poor unhappy Beata into the mill-race.

Rebecca. Yes—it was like a fight for life between Beata and me at that time.

Rosmer. You proved the strongest of us all at Rosmersholm—stronger than both Beata and me put together.

Rebecca. I knew you well enough to know that I could not get at you in any way until you were set free—both in actual circumstances and in your soul.

Rosmer. But I do not understand you, Rebecca. You—you yourself and your whole conduct—are an insoluble riddle to me. I am free now—both in my soul and my circumstances. You are absolutely in touch with the goal you set before yourself from the beginning. And nevertheless—

Rebecca. I have never stood farther from my goal than I do now.

Rosmer. And nevertheless, I say, when yesterday I asked you—urged you—to become my wife, you cried out that it never could be.

Rebecca. I cried out in despair, John.

Rosmer. Why?

Rebecca. Because Rosmersholm has unnerved me. All the courage has been sapped out of my will here—crushed out! The time has gone for me to dare risk anything whatever. I have lost all power of action, John.

Rosmer. Tell me how that has come about.

Rebecca. It has come about through my living with you.

Rosmer. But how? How?

Rebecca. When I was alone with you here—and you had really found yourself—

Rosmer. Yes, yes?

Rebecca. For you never really found yourself as long as Beata was Alive—

Rosmer. Alas, you are right in that.

Rebecca. When it came about that I was living together with you here, in peace and solitude—when you exchanged all your thoughts with me unreservedly—your every mood, however tender or intimate—then the great change happened in me. Little by little, you understand. Almost imperceptibly—but overwhelmingly in the end, till it reached the uttermost depths of my soul.

Rosmer. What does this mean, Rebecca?

Rebecca. All the other feeling—all that horrible passion that had drowned my better self—left me entirely. All the violent emotions that had been roused in me were quelled and silenced. A peace stole over my soul—a quiet like that of one of our mountain peaks up under the midnight sun.

Rosmer. Tell me more of it—all that you can.

Rebecca. There is not much more to tell. Only that this was how love grew up in my heart—a great, self-denying love—content with such a union of hearts as there has been between us two.

Rosmer. Oh, if only I had had the slightest suspicion of all this!

Rebecca. It is best as it is. Yesterday, when you asked me if I would be your wife, I gave a cry of joy—

Rosmer. Yes, it was that, Rebecca, was it not! I thought that was what it meant.

Rebecca. For a moment, yes-I forgot myself for a moment. It was my dauntless will of the old days that was struggling to be free again. But now it has no more strength—it has lost it for ever.

Rosmer. How do you explain what has taken place in you?

Rebecca. It is the Rosmer attitude towards life-or your attitude towards life, at any rate—that has infected my will.

Rosmer. Infected?

Rebecca. Yes, and made it sickly—bound it captive under laws that formerly had no meaning for me. You—my life together with you—have ennobled my soul—

Rosmer. Ah, if I dared believe that to be true!

Rebecca. You may believe it confidently. The Rosmer attitude towards life ennobles. But-(shakes her head)-but-but—

Rosmer. But? Well?

Rebecca. But it kills joy, you know.

Rosmer. Do you say that, Rebecca?

Rebecca. For me, at all events.

Rosmer. Yes, but are you so sure of that? If I asked you again now—? Implored you—?

Rebecca. Oh, my dear—never go back to that again! It is impossible. Yes, impossible—because I must tell you this, John. I have a—past behind me.

Rosmer. Something more than you have told me?

Rebecca. Yes, something more and something different.

Rosmer (with a faint smile). It is very strange, Rebecca, but—do you know—the idea of such a thing has occurred to me more than once.

Rebecca. It has? And yet—notwithstanding that, you—?

Rosmer. I never believed in it. I only played with the idea-nothing more.

Rebecca. If you wish, I will tell you all about it at once.

Rosmer (stopping her). No, no! I do not want to hear a word about it. Whatever it is, it shall be forgotten, as far as I am concerned.

Rebecca. But I cannot forget it.

Rosmer. Oh, Rebecca—!

Rebecca. Yes, dear—that is just the dreadful part of it-that now, when all the happiness of life is freely and fully offered to me, all I can feel is that I am barred out from it by my past.

Rosmer. Your past is dead, Rebecca. It has no longer any hold on you—has nothing to do with you—as you are now.

Rebecca. Ah, my dear, those are mere words, you know. What about innocence, then? Where am I to get that from?

Rosmer (gloomily). Ah, yes—innocence.

Rebecca. Yes, innocence—which is at the root of all joy and happiness. That was the teaching, you know, that you wanted to see realised by all the men you were going to raise up to nobility and happiness.

Rosmer. Ah, do not remind me of that. It was nothing but a half-dreamt dream, Rebecca—a rash suggestion that I have no longer any faith in. Human nature cannot be ennobled by outside influences, believe me.

Rebecca (gently). Not by a tranquil love, do you think?

Rosmer (thoughtfully). Yes, that would be a splendid thing—almost the most glorious thing in life, I think if it were so. (Moves restlessly.) But how am I ever to clear up the question?—how am I to get to the bottom of it?

Rebecca. Do you not believe in me, John?

Rosmer. Ah, Rebecca, how can I believe you entirely—you whose life here has been nothing but continual concealment and secrecy!—And now you have this new tale to tell. If it is cloaking some design of yours, tell me so—openly. Perhaps there is something or other that you hope to gain by that means? I will gladly do anything that I can for you.

Rebecca (wringing her hands). Oh, this killing doubt! John, John—!

Rosmer. Yes, I know, dear—it is horrible—but I cannot help it. I shall never be able to free myself from it—never be able to feel certain that your love for me is genuine and pure.

Rebecca. But is there nothing in your own heart that bears witness to the transformation that has taken place in me—and taken place through your influence, and yours alone!

Rosmer. Ah, my dear, I do not believe any longer in my power to transform people. I have no belief in myself left at all. I do not believe either in myself or in you.

Rebecca (looking darkly at him). How are you going to live out your life, then?

Rosmer. That is just what I do not know—and cannot imagine. I do not believe I can live it out. And, moreover, I do not know anything in the world that would be worth living for.

Rebecca. Life carries a perpetual rebirth with it. Let us hold fast to it, dear. We shall be finished with it quite soon enough.

Rosmer (getting up restlessly). Then give me my faith back again!—my faith in you, Rebecca—my faith in your love! Give me a proof of it! I must have some proof!

Rebecca. Proof? How can I give you a proof—!

Rosmer. You must! (Crosses the room.) I cannot bear this desolate, horrible loneliness—this-this—. (A knock is heard at the hall door.)

Rebecca (getting up from her chair). Did you hear that?

(The door opens, and ULRIK BRENDEL comes in. Except that he wears a white shirt, a black coat and, a good pair of high boots, he is dressed as in the first act. He looks troubled.)

Rosmer. Ah, it is you, Mr. Brendel!

Brendel. John, my boy, I have come to say good-bye to you!

Rosmer. Where are you going, so late as this?

Brendel. Downhill.

Rosmer. How—?

Brendel. I am on my way home, my beloved pupil. I am homesick for the great Nothingness.

Rosmer. Something has happened to you, Mr. Brendel! What is it?

Brendel. Ah, you notice the transformation, then? Well, it is evident enough. The last time I entered your doors I stood before you a man of substance, slapping a well-filled pocket.

Rosmer. Really? I don't quite understand—

Brendel. And now, as you see me to-night, I am a deposed monarch standing over the ashes of my burnt-out palace.

Rosmer. If there is any way I can help you

Brendel. You have preserved your childlike heart, John—can you let me have a loan?

Rosmer. Yes, most willingly!

Brendel. Can you spare me an ideal or two?

Rosmer. What do you say?

Brendel. One or two cast-off ideals? You will be doing a good deed. I am cleaned out, my dear boy, absolutely and entirely.

Rebecca. Did you not succeed in giving your lecture?

Brendel. No, fair lady. What do you think?—just as I was standing ready to pour out the contents of my horn in plenty, I made the painful discovery that I was bankrupt.

Rebecca. But what of all your unwritten works, then?

Brendel. For five and twenty years I have been like a miser sitting on his locked money-chest. And then to-day, when I opened it to take out my treasure—there was nothing there! The mills of time had ground it into dust. There was not a blessed thing left of the whole lot.

Rosmer. But are you certain of that?

Brendel. There is no room for doubt, my dear boy. The President has convinced me of that.

Rosmer. The President?

Brendel. Oh, well—His Excellency, then. Ganz nach Belieben.

Rosmer. But whom do you mean?

Brendel. Peter Mortensgaard, of course.

Rosmer. What!

Brendel (mysteriously). Hush, hush, hush! Peter Mortensgaard is Lord and Chieftain of the Future. I have never stood in a more august presence. Peter Mortensgaard has the power of omnipotence in him. He can do whatever he wants.

Rosmer. Oh, come—don't you believe that!

Brendel. It is true, my boy—because Peter Mortensgaard never wants to do more than he can. Peter Mortensgaard is capable of living his life without ideals. And that, believe me, is precisely the great secret of success in life. It sums up all the wisdom of the world. Basta!

Rosmer (in a low voice). Now I see that you are going away from here poorer than you came.

Brendel. Bien! Then take an example from your old tutor. Erase from your mind everything that he imprinted there. Do not build your castle upon the shifting sand. And look well ahead, and be sure of your ground, before you build upon the charming creature who is sweetening your life here.

Rebecca. Do you mean me?

Brendel. Yes, most attractive mermaid!

Rebecca. Why am I not fit to build upon?

Brendel (taking a step nearer to her). I understood that my former pupil had a cause which it was his life's work to lead to victory.

Rebecca. And if he has—?

Brendel. He is certain of victory—but, be it distinctly understood, on one unalterable condition.

Rebecca. What is that?

Brendel (taking her gently by the wrist). That the woman who loves him shall gladly go out into the kitchen and chop off her dainty, pink and white little finger—here, just at the middle joint. Furthermore, that the aforesaid loving woman shall—also gladly—clip off her incomparably moulded left ear. (Lets her go, and turns to ROSMER.) Good-bye, John the Victorious!

Rosmer. Must you go now—in this dark night?

Brendel. The dark night is best. Peace be with you! (He goes out. Silence in the room for a short time.)

Rebecca (breathing heavily). How close and sultry it is in here! (Goes to the window, opens it and stands by it.)

Rosmer (sitting down on a chair by the stove). There is nothing else for it after all, Rebecca—I can see that. You must go away.

Rebecca. Yes, I do not see that I have any choice.

Rosmer. Let us make use of our last hour together. Come over here and sit beside me.

Rebecca (goes and sits down on the couch). What do you want, John?

Rosmer. In the first place I want to tell you that you need have no anxiety about your future.

Rebecca (with a smile). Hm! My future!

Rosmer. I have foreseen all contingencies—long ago. Whatever may happen, you are provided for.

Rebecca. Have you even done that for me, dear?

Rosmer. You might have known that I should.

Rebecca. It is many a long day since I thought about anything of the kind.

Rosmer. Yes, of course. Naturally, you thought things could never be otherwise between us than as they were.

Rebecca. Yes, that was what I thought.

Rosmer. So did I. But if anything were to happen to me now—

Rebecca. Oh, John, you will live longer than I shall.

Rosmer. I can dispose of my miserable existence as I please, you know.

Rebecca. What do you mean? You surely are never thinking of—!

Rosmer. Do you think it would be so surprising? After the pitiful, lamentable defeat I have suffered? I, who was to have made it my life's work to lead my cause to victory—! And here I am, a deserter before the fight has even really begun!

Rebecca. Take up the fight again, John! Only try—and you will see that you will conquer. You will ennoble hundreds—thousands—of souls. Only try!

Rosmer. I, Rebecca, who no longer believe even in my having a mission in life?

Rebecca. But your mission has stood the test. You have at all events ennobled one of your fellow-creatures for the rest of her life—I mean myself.

Rosmer. Yes—if I dared believe you about that.

Rebecca (wringing her hands). But, John, do you know of nothing—nothing—that would make you believe that?

Rosmer (starts, as if with fear). Don't venture on that subject! No further, Rebecca! Not a single word more!

Rebecca. Indeed, that is just the subject we must venture upon. Do you know of anything that would stifle your doubts? For I know of nothing in the world.

Rosmer. It is best for you not to know. Best for us both.

Rebecca. No, no, no—I have no patience with that sort of thing! If you know of anything that would acquit me in your eyes, I claim it as my right that you should name it.

Rosmer (as if impelled against his will). Well, let us see. You say that you have great love in your heart; that your soul has been ennobled through me. Is that so? Have you counted the cost? Shall we try and balance our accounts? Tell me.

Rebecca. I am quite ready.

Rosmer. Then when shall it be?

Rebecca. Whenever you like. The sooner the better.

Rosmer. Then let me see, Rebecca, whether you—for my sake-this very night—. (Breaks off.) Oh, no, no!

Rebecca. Yes, John! Yes, yes! Say it, and you shall see.

Rosmer. Have you the courage—are you willing—gladly, as Ulrik Brendel said—for my sake, to-night—gladly—to go the same way—that Beata went!

Rebecca (gets up slowly from the couch, and says almost inaudibly): John—!

Rosmer. Yes, dear—that is the question I shall never be able to rid my thoughts of, when you have gone away. Every hour of the day I shall come back to it. Ah, I seem to see you bodily before me—standing out on the foot-bridge-right out in the middle. Now you lean out over the railing! You grow dizzy as you feel drawn down towards the mill-race! No—you recoil. You dare not do—what she dared.

Rebecca. But if I had the courage?—and willingly and gladly? What then?

Rosmer. Then I would believe in you. Then I should get back my faith in my mission in life—my faith in my power to ennoble my fellow men—my faith in mankind's power to be ennobled.

Rebecca (takes up her shawl slowly, throws it over her head, and says, controlling herself): You shall have your faith back.

Rosmer. Have you the courage and the strength of will for that, Rebecca?

Rebecca. Of that you must judge in the morning—or later—when they take up my body.

Rosmer (burying his head in his hands). There is a horrible temptation in this—!

Rebecca. Because I should not like to be left lying there—any longer than need be. You must take care that they find me.

Rosmer (springing up). But all this is madness, you know. Go away, or stay! I will believe you on your bare word this time too.

Rebecca. Those are mere words, John. No more cowardice or evasion! How can you believe me on my bare word after today?

Rosmer. But I do not want to see your defeat, Rebecca.

Rebecca. There will be no defeat.

Rosmer. There will. You will never have the heart to go Beata's way.

Rebecca. Do you believe that?

Rosmer. Never. You are not like Beata. You are not under the influence of a distorted view of life.

Rebecca. But I am under the influence of the Rosmersholm view of Life—now. Whatever my offences are—it is right that I should expiate them.

Rosmer (looking at her fixedly). Have you come to that decision?

Rebecca. Yes.

Rosmer. Very well. Then I too am under the influence of our unfettered view of life, Rebecca. There is no one that can judge us. And therefore we must be our own judges.

Rebecca (misunderstanding his meaning). That too. That too. My leaving you will save the best that is in you.

Rosmer. Ah, there is nothing left to save in me.

Rebecca. There is. But I—after this I should only be like some sea-sprite hanging on to the barque you are striving to sail forward in, and, hampering its progress. I must go overboard. Do you think I could go through the world bearing the burden of a spoiled life—brooding for ever over the happiness which I have forfeited by my past? I must throw up the game, John.

Rosmer. If you go—then I go with you.

Rebecca (looks at him with an almost imperceptible smile, and says more gently): Yes, come with me, dear—and be witness—

Rosmer. I go with you, I said.

Rebecca. As far as the bridge—yes. You never dare go out on to it, you know.

Rosmer. Have you noticed that?

Rebecca (in sad and broken tones). Yes. That was what made my love hopeless.

Rosmer. Rebecca—now I lay my hand on your head. (Does as he says.) And I take you for my true and lawful wife.

Rebecca (taking both his hands in hers, and bowing her head on to his breast). Thank you, John. (Lets him go.) And now I am going—gladly.

Rosmer. Man and wife should go together.

Rebecca. Only as far as the bridge, John.

Rosmer. And out on to it, too. As far as you go—so far I go with you. I dare do it now.

Rebecca. Are you absolutely certain that way is the best for you?

Rosmer. I know it is the only way.

Rebecca. But suppose you are only deceiving yourself? Suppose it were only a delusion—one of these White Horses of Rosmersholm?

Rosmer. It may be so. We can never escape from them—we of my race.

Rebecca. Then stay, John!

Rosmer. The man shall cleave to his wife, as the wife to her husband.

Rebecca. Yes, but first tell me this—is it you that go with me, or I that go with you?

Rosmer. We shall never get to the bottom of that.

Rebecca. Yet I should dearly like to know.

Rosmer. We two go with each other, Rebecca. I with you, and you with me.

Rebecca. I almost believe that is true.

Rosmer. For now we two are one.

Rebecca. Yes. We are one now. Come! We can go gladly now. (They go out, hand in hand, through the hall, and are seen to turn to the left. The door stands open after them. The room is empty for a little while. Then MRS. HELSETH opens the door on the right.)

Mrs. Helseth. The carriage, miss, is—. (Looks round the room.) Not here? Out together at this time of night? Well, well—I must say—! Hm! (Goes out into the hall, looks round and comes in again.) Not sitting on the bench—ah, well! (Goes to the window and looks out.) Good heavens! What is that white thing—! As I am a living soul, they are both out on the foot-bridge! God forgive the sinful creatures—if they are not in each other's arms! (Gives a wild scream.) Ah!—they are over—both of them! Over into the mill-race! Help! help! (Her knees tremble, she holds on shakily to the back of a chair and can scarcely get her words out.) No. No help here. The dead woman has taken them.